*Dedicated to those who live on in our memories.*

WEREWOLF UNDYING: A HEARTBLAZE NOVEL

# HARD LANDING

## ASH KINLEY

WE STAND TOGETHER under a stunning night sky. Above, I see the burning eye of the Wolf Head constellation, cloaked by the swaying green-and-white northern lights above Norway.

It feels like I'm falling. I hold tightly on to Stefan and Tyler's hands. But we're not really falling, we're beginning to time travel. The aurora jumps into rapid motion, as if panicked.

At last, we're returning to Corby! Once there, I hope I'll be able to invoke Seeker, my wolf. I'm also hoping to find Shasta and Lucky, my two lost dogs. I didn't locate them here in medieval Norway, so it's possible they never crossed the time rift, and they're still in the woods outside Corby.

My time in the Viking era was terrifying. But thankfully, Gríma was killed and Seeker was saved. With any luck, Gríma did not disrupt the timeline and we'll find Corby as we left it. But I don't like our chances. Gríma introduced guns to the Norse world, and who knows if we collected them all? Could those guns affect our modern world? We'll know soon enough.

The falling sensation suddenly becomes more intense, much worse than the first time I jumped with Tyler.

Tyler's grip on my hand tightens, causing a spasm of pain. His eyes widen with shock. Something is wrong.

Stefan's grip weakens and I see his head slump. Is he passing out?

I cry out in pain. It feels like I'm being stretched. My muscles and joints burn and my skin threatens to split open.

The rugged, icy world around us fades away and I catch a hazy glimpse of people using picks to chip ice from the side of a frozen, misty mountain. The workers have pale blue skin. Are they dead? Some have rope burns around their necks. Were they hanged?

What is this place? It couldn't possibly be Corby.

I glance over at Tyler. His eyes are closed in concentration.

I call out to him, "What's happening?" But my voice emerges high-pitched and barely audible. Tyler doesn't seem to hear me.

Stefan falls to his knees, his hand limp in mine. Blood, from somewhere under the sleeve of his fur tunic, runs down his arm and onto our hands. I want desperately to help him, but I can't release Tyler's hand in the middle of a time jump.

I exhale in relief as the frozen mountain disappears, replaced by the familiar forest outside of Corby. We made it!

Tyler releases my hand, collapsing to the woodland floor.

A wave of nausea washes over me and I stumble to keep my balance. The assault rifle I took from one of Gríma's crew, hanging on my shoulder from a strap, slips to the ground.

The air is smoky, and I can't help but cough.

Somehow, I've managed to hold on to Stefan's bloody hand. He lies on the ground, semiconscious. Tyler looks completely knocked out.

Stefan watches me through half-open eyes, whispering something I can't hear. I remove his shoulder holster and handgun, then peel off his tunic. I see a set of bleeding runes carved into his forearm.

# ᛗᚠᚺᛏᚠ

"Stefan, what happened?"

He grits his teeth, managing a few words. "Mahna ... tried ... to hold me."

In the days that followed my reunion with Stefan, he told me about Mahna, the powerful witch who took over his body and tried to kill me. Something told me we hadn't seen the last of her.

I don't have anything to clean and bind Stefan's wound. Maybe Tyler does.

I step over to Tyler's unconscious body. He's bitten his forked tongue and a bit of blood has trickled over his lip. His dracoform skin is waxy and hot to the touch. He's breathing, and his heart is beating. He probably passed out from the shock of the rough journey. He was doing all the work.

I shake him gently. "Tyler? Tyler, are you all right?"

He doesn't respond. Behind me, Stefan groans as he pushes himself into a sitting position, his entire body trembling. He sniffs the air and mutters, "Smoke. Not good."

I pull my cell phone from my pouch and hit the power switch, but it doesn't come on. "Stefan, is your phone working?"

He nods to his pouch. I remove his phone, frowning after I turn it on. "No signal."

Stefan doesn't react. Something tells me the damage he suffered extends beyond his arm.

I return his phone to his pouch.

Tyler has a pouch at his waist, now half-hidden by his body. I roll him over and open it.

I feel another wave of nausea as I reach into the pouch and my arm disappears up to my elbow, then up to my shoulder. The pouch looks to be about six inches deep, but inside it's the size of a car trunk, maybe even bigger. How is that possible?

I find many things inside the pouch: Tyler's crystal claws, phone, slender bars of gold and silver, a canteen, flashlight, utility knife, portable water purifier, small tent, a pair of inflatable camping mattresses, axe, wood saw, various types of firestarters, folding shovel, cooking and eating utensils, small propane stove with fuel, crossbow with a set of bolts, fishing gear, scoped hunting handgun with a long barrel and spare ammo, binoculars, a wide assortment of dried and freeze-dried foods, spare clothes and shoes, space blanket, an excellent medical kit complete

with prescription-strength antibiotics and painkillers, dozens of condoms, and finally, a mysterious fist-sized cube of polished metal.

Wow. Tyler really comes prepared. How is all this fitting inside the pouch? Clearly, it's no ordinary pouch. It doesn't feel like it weighs more than a pound. There must be magic at work here.

I turn on Tyler's phone, but it's not showing a signal either.

I use the medical kit to clean and bind Stefan's arm wound. His eyes never leave Tyler's pouch. He's clearly intrigued by it, but says nothing.

Stefan drinks from the canteen, accepting the antibiotics but refusing the painkillers. I think about forcing some antibiotics into Tyler, but he doesn't have any apparent wounds.

I wonder if Stefan's wolf will help his wounded arm heal faster. Does he have his wolf? With a sharp pang, I realize I don't have mine. Seeker is still unreachable.

"Stefan, can you invoke?"

He shakes his head grimly.

A sinking feeling threatens to overwhelm me and I plop down on the ground beside Stefan. Something's gone horribly wrong. Saving Seeker's life back in the Viking era was supposed to ensure she would survive into modern times. Now that we're back in Corby, Stefan and I should be able to invoke.

Does this mean that Seeker died after all? Or has Gríma done something in the past that radically changed our present?

I grab the rifle and turn to Stefan. "I'll head into Corby and get help. Can you keep an eye on Tyler? He's passed out, but I'm hoping he'll wake up."

Stefan frowns, annoyed at being incapacitated. "Find Cain. See if he knows the source of the smoke. But be careful. Keep checking for the rift."

I suddenly remember the time compass Stefan gave me. I pull it out and we look at the compass face. The silver needle is motionless and the gold needle points at me.

I meet his eyes. "That's good, right?"

He nods. "Maybe the rift is gone. But keep checking."

I hug Stefan goodbye, then stand on aching legs, looking around to get my bearings. I recognize the forest around our landing zone and know exactly where to find Corby.

My body hurts so much that I can barely walk. I nod to Stefan and set off toward Corby. I glance back and he returns a pained look. It must be killing him that he's not fit to travel. But at least someone is here to keep watch over Tyler.

As I move into the woods, I notice that a fine layer of soot covers the needles of the pine trees and the leaves of the shrubs. I'm guessing this smoke has been here for a while.

Despite my aching legs, I find myself picking up the pace. I'm eager to get into Corby and find help for Stefan and Tyler.

Part of me wants to call out to find my dogs, but it's probably better to remain silent. I don't know if I'm safe here. I have the assault rifle for protection, and also my slingshot and lead pellets. But what I don't have is the Heartstone, given to me by the goddess Skadi. It was lost in the battle with Gríma. Looking into the silent shadows of the forest, I wish I still had that stone, for peace of mind if nothing else. Does Skadi still watch over me here in the present?

In less than five minutes, I make my way to where Corby ought to be.

There's nothing but trees!

This looks like the right area, based on the stream and the low, rolling hills. But the trees have never been cleared out to build a town. What the hell happened to Corby?

My gut clenches and I take a deep breath of smoky air, trying not to panic.

Maybe I got the location wrong. The trees are thick here. I need a better vantage point.

I walk to the top of a rise, hide my rifle under some bushes, and find the tallest tree. It should give me a good view of the entire area. I'd actually like to take the rifle, but it'd be tough to get it through the thick branches of the tree.

The climb is strange. Although I'm sore, I can climb without tiring. I've put on some muscle in the last couple of weeks and it shows. I finally get high enough to have a good look around. I can see for miles and miles. There's no sign of any town.

My heart sinks. This is bad. Gríma must have somehow altered the timeline, and now Corby doesn't exist.

In the distance to the west I can see Mount Mansfield. Its outline looks vaguely like the profile of a human face. Something is wrong there. I see smoke drifting up from the mountain. Is it on fire?

Then I realize it's not a fire. The mountain is volcanic, and it's probably the source of the smoke spread across the area.

Did Tyler get confused during the time jump? Instead of taking us to the present, did he take us to the distant past? Is this Stone Age Vermont?

Pulse quickening, I scramble down the tree, adrenaline masking the pain in my body.

When I reach the ground, I feel a brief temptation to visit my shack. My dogs may have returned there. But it's six miles away, and I don't want to leave Stefan and Tyler alone for that long. Besides, in my heart I know the shack won't be there, and neither will my dogs.

I retrieve the rifle and start to run back to the place where I left Stefan and Tyler, coughing as I take in heavy breaths of smoky air.

Eyes watering, I force myself to stop and take a reading from the time compass. Still no sign of the rift. That's the only piece of good news to be found.

I stow the compass in my pouch and continue running toward our landing zone. I have to find a way to wake Tyler up so he can get us out of here.

When I finally arrive, gasping for air, Stefan and Tyler are gone!

# Redbeard

## STEFAN HILDEBRAND

MY HEAD RINGS like a hammer on an anvil, each strike sending a wave of pain through my temples. But the pain isn't the worst part; more troubling are the exhaustion and confusion.

After Ash leaves for Corby, I find another set of pills in Tempus's medical kit. Damn, not Tempus, Tyler. I have to remember to call him by his real name now.

Ash probably didn't recognize these pills, but I know *modafinil* from my time with the Knights of Rome. KoR and other military forces use it as a "go pill." It promotes wakefulness and clear thinking without the risks of amphetamines. I wash down a pair of the pills using water from Tyler's canteen.

Waiting for the modafinil to kick in, I mentally review my wild ride back from the Viking era. I almost didn't make it. My connection to Mahna acted like an anchor, binding me to her in the past. I could feel Tyler fighting her as my body threatened to tear itself apart.

I remember catching a mist-shrouded glimpse of Mahna with an ice pick in her hand. She looked dead, or rather, undead. Was she in Norse hell? If so, I hope she stays there.

When we arrived here in the present, my connection with her broke. I hope I'm free of her now. Whatever she did to me happened over a thousand years in the past, and thousands of miles away. The runes she carved in my arm, spelling out her name, have stopped bleeding, and the pain is already fading away.

Feeling a little stronger, I put my tunic and shoulder holster back on, then crawl over to examine Tyler. He has no obvious injuries, but I think something broke inside him as he pulled me from Mahna's grasp. I owe him for getting me here.

I tilt the canteen to his mouth and manage to get a little water into him. He's still unconscious, but his swallowing reflexes are working. He may have internal injuries. I need to get him to the hospital in Burlington. There's a paranormal-friendly doctor there who has helped my father.

An image of Magnus creeps into my mind. My gut twists as I remember him lying boneless in the snow. Time travel is dangerous. I really hope Tyler survives this.

I climb unsteadily to my feet and take a good look around. I recognize this part of the woods. We're just outside of Corby. But what's with all the smoke? Has KoR released another one of their smoke weapons, like the one that stripped us of our wolves? Maybe that's why I don't have my wolf here. I've been unable to invoke for so long, I'm getting used to it. That depresses me.

My instincts tell me it isn't safe here, and I curse myself for letting Ash go to Corby alone.

We're out here in an exposed position. I want to move Tyler to a more secure spot that overlooks this area. That way I can spot Ash when she returns. But if Tyler has internal injuries, moving him could make them worse. It's a tough call, but I'm gonna go with my instinct and change our position.

I return all of Tyler's items to his magic pouch. When he wakes up, I should ask him how to get one of those for myself.

I lift Tyler into a fireman's carry, and I almost collapse under his weight. I still don't have my full strength, but I need to do this.

Taking one shaky step after another, I slowly make my way up a low hill. At the top is a small rock face, hidden in the shadow of a towering hemlock tree. It's a defensible position with a commanding view, and the thick tree canopy will diffuse the telltale smoke of a campfire.

It's less than a hundred yards, but I arrive soaked in sweat and drop Tyler harder than I intended. He doesn't react.

A cool fall breeze, laced with the bitter smoke, blows over my wet skin, chilling me. I need to stay active until I dry off.

I use Tyler's folding shovel to dig a pit for a fire. A recessed fire will be almost impossible to spot. Help from Corby will probably be arriving soon, but it's better to be safe than sorry, and I need something to focus on.

The modafinil is starting to kick in and I feel good enough to gather some wood for the fire. I won't light it yet, but I want it to be ready. After gathering some dried branches and twigs, I arrange them in the pit, all the while keeping an eye out for Ash.

What's with the layer of soot on the trees and plants in the area? It makes me think this smoke has been around for a long time. I'm not sure what that means, but it's nothing good.

Ash should be back by now. I wonder what's keeping her. I wish our phones were working.

I check my phone again, but there's still no signal. I also pull Tyler's phone from his pouch and check it. No luck there either.

As I return Tyler's phone to his pouch, I notice a gleaming cube about four inches on each side. I take it out of the pouch to examine it. The metal looks like chrome, but it feels too light for that. Faint etchings decorate the cube. They look vaguely like circuits, but seem to be worn down by many years of polishing.

Tyler's pouch is clearly a magical device, but I'm not so sure about the cube. It could be technological. If I had to make a wild guess, I'd say it's some sort of satellite transmitter or receiver. Is it something I could use to summon help?

I tense as I catch movement in the corner of my eye. I draw my Glock and turn to see Ash emerging from the trees at our original position. She looks stunned for a moment, until I whistle to get her attention. She scrambles up the hill to join us.

I holster my weapon, annoyed by my own jumpiness. Is that a side effect of the modafinil?

I put the cube away as Ash joins me, her face pinched with worry. "Corby isn't there!"

I take a moment to digest her words. "What do you mean, exactly?"

"There's no sign that Corby was ever built. And Mount Mansfield is a volcano. I think it's the source of the smoke. I'm wondering if we're actually in the past, like the Stone Age. That would explain the lack of cell signal."

*Shit. So much for getting Tyler to a hospital.*

I nod my head. "Had a feeling something wasn't right here. I think Mahna screwed up Tyler's time jump."

Ash crouches next to Tyler and squeezes his hand. "Has he moved? Said anything?"

I shake my head. "He once said he needs to rest after a jump. I hope that's what he's doing."

Ash looks out at the imposing forest. "What should we do?"

"Survive. Until Tyler wakes up. Then try another jump. Hey, when you were out, did you see any signs of people?"

Ash shakes her head. "I was focused on looking for buildings. But I didn't see any people or tracks."

I rummage around in Tyler's pack until I find the water filter and a handful of condoms.

Ash laughs. "I can't imagine what you're planning."

"The condoms are unlubricated. They're for gathering water. Tyler has tea, coffee, and freeze-dried food. With water, we can make a hot meal and get our strength back."

Ash nods. "That sounds good."

"I'll be back soon. Keep your rifle in hand and your eyes downslope."

Ash's face shows concern. "Be careful, Stefan, you still look pale."

I nod and give her a quick smile, grabbing the canteen as I go.

Heading down the hill, I feel a little guilty for not revealing my full intentions for this hike.

As I advance into the trees, I take one last glance back at Ash. She's crouched beside Tyler, ready to shoot anything that moves. Good. We could be in unfriendly territory. It's important to stay alert.

I admire Ash. She's brave and strong. And I trust her too. But I need to see Corby, or the lack of it, with my own eyes. After a few minutes of hiking I reach a place that should be on the outskirts of town.

There's nothing here but trees.

This area was never cleared for development. I start to scale a tree for a better look around and quickly discover that my body's not up to that yet.

Suppressing a dull sense of dread, I hike south until I reach the stream that should run past Redbeard, the tree that Ash and I were drawn to at different times in our lives.

This will be the test. If Redbeard isn't there, we are probably in the past.

I spot the tree ahead, not knowing whether to feel fear or relief. As I get close I see the red patch in the shape of a beard where the bark is missing.

Not long ago, Ash and I stood together here, looking at where we scratched our names into this tree. But now, the names are nowhere to be seen.

We aren't in the past. We're in the present. A present where Corby doesn't exist. A present where Ash and I may never have been born.

A chill passes through me. It was that fucking Gríma. We killed her, but she had already done something to mess up the timeline. Now we have to figure out what it was, and fix it. Everything hinges on Tyler now. He needs to wake up soon.

Kneeling beside the stream, I use the water filter to pump clean water into the canteen and condoms. The condoms swell up like water balloons.

I try to focus on the task, but my mind wanders. Corby is gone. But what if the problem is bigger than Corby? I've seen no signs of life. What if mankind no longer exists? What if Gríma triggered some sort of apocalyptic event that wiped everyone out?

As I tie off the last condom, I notice something in the mud on the opposite side of the stream. I cross the shallow water for a closer look.

Footprints!

These prints appear human. They're small, as if made by a child's shoes. Except something is off. The heels are too narrow, and the balls too wide. If these are human prints, they were made by someone deformed.

Suddenly, I think of Ash, holding down the camp on her own. I need to warn her, to be there with her.

Clutching the canteen, filter, and water-filled condoms, I race through the trees, desperate to reach Ash before something else does.

## CRASH CUBE

### TYLER BUCK

THIS JUMP IS GOING SIDEWAYS. I'm expecting to see the forests of Corby, but instead I see a chain gang of Norse zombies chipping ice off a mist-covered mountain.

And then there's the pain, like getting kicked in the balls, only I feel it throughout my whole body.

Ash's grip on my left hand is strong, but Stefan's grip on my right is weakening. We're under attack and he is the target.

I think I know what's happening. In the days after Gríma's death, when Stefan was recovering from his leg wound, he talked about Mahna, the witch who switched bodies with him. He managed to kill her, but maybe their souls are somehow tied together.

I think I recognize this frozen land filled with undead. I've never been here, but it was described to me at the Time Academy, in my class on Norse cosmology.

This place is probably Niflheim, or Helheim, depending on the source. It's the lowest, scariest world in the Norse worlds, the closest thing they have to a hell. Mahna is trapped here, and she wants Stefan to join her.

I've never made such a difficult jump, and it can end in several ways, depending on the decision I make right now.

I can drop Stefan and complete the jump with Ash. That would be the safest option.

I can abort the jump and return to our exit point in medieval Norway. But the tether on Stefan will still exist, so it will be just as hard going back as going forward.

The last option is to fight the witch's magic. But I would have to go all in. If I fail, we all could die, or be scattered in the winds of time, never to reconnect with each other.

My instinct is to fight, but what do Ash and Stefan want? There's no way I can ask them. I'll just have to decide for all of us.

I can see Mahna now, with a pickaxe in her pale hand. She's just as Stefan described, dark hair braided on one side and loose on the other. She seems to sense us, her grin exposing a green gem set in her front tooth.

Oh, *it's on*, you clingy Norse bitch.

I close my eyes, putting everything I have into completing the jump.

I feel something break.

The pain is unbelievable, like someone picking the meat from my bones using rusty tweezers. I want to scream, but I can't afford to waste the energy.

For some reason, I can't find the anchor I left outside of Corby, the mental homing beacon that lets me cross the physical space between Norway and Corby.

I'll just do my best to finish this jump, but I'm already starting to lose consciousness.

For a moment, I smell pine trees and sour smoke. Then everything fades away.

I wake up inside *the room*.

I've heard a lot about this place, but I've never seen it in person. No one wants to see it in person. If you land here, it means you took a jump that hurt you bad.

It's a small room with two hardwood chairs on each side of a low table. Three crystal spheres rest in depressions on the table: one red, one green, and one blue.

I fall into a chair, not bothering to look for a door. This room doesn't have an exit.

This room is my crash cube. I'm trapped in here like a genie in a bottle. A sense of dread and claustrophobia threatens to overwhelm me. I need to put my feelings aside and focus on the situation.

Every agent of Specta Aeternal carries a crash cube, designed to protect them when a jump goes wrong. It's a small metal cube made from a substance not found on this earth. It's not a particularly hard metal, but it's lightweight and holds magic with almost no residual loss over time. No one will tell you what metal it's made from. At the Time Academy, we jokingly call it *unobtainium*.

The body I have inside this cube is an illusion, an avatar. My real body is probably lying unconscious in the forest outside of Corby. I hope someone will keep the ants off me. Ants really bother me for some reason.

I barely remember the class I received on interpreting the three crystal spheres before me. I wish I'd paid more attention.

The blue sphere represents the current state of my body. The red is my mind, and the green my soul.

I closely examine the colored spheres, all glowing with light. Each is filled with a complex network of bright veins, like some sort of artificial brain.

Half of the veins in the blue sphere have darkened. That means my body is dying. The red sphere is more or less intact, so I still have most of my memories and intelligence. But the green sphere is three-quarters dark, indicating my soul is almost dead.

It looks like I received a traumatic metaphysical injury fighting off Mahna's magic. Once the soul is hurt this badly, the injury starts to affect the flesh. So not all of the harm done to my body is due to the wild jump; some of it is collateral damage from the metaphysical wound.

Long story short, without the help of a skilled metaphysician, I don't have long to live. The damage to my soul will likely remain stable at this point, but my body will go downhill fast.

I should consider myself lucky. If I wasn't a dracoform, and tougher than a normal human, I'd already be dead, and the jump would have failed. Ash and Stefan could have ended up chipping ice with Mahna in Helheim.

When my body eventually dies, my mind will still be safe inside the crash cube. A distress beacon is already transmitting from the cube, and my fellow agents in Specta Aeternal should be able to recover it. Worst-case scenario, they'll patch up my soul and put my mind into a new body.

Something isn't right here, and I finally realize what it is.

I stare at the empty chair across from me. That's really bad.

When a crash cube is triggered, an avatar of the SA bureau chief from the local era should appear in that chair to debrief me.

Specta Aeternal doesn't just abandon their highly trained operatives. If they're not here, they may not know about my mishap. The cube might be faulty, or damaged.

But something even worse could have happened. If I'm on a rogue timeline, one that got rewoven by Gríma's actions in the past, Specta Aeternal *may not exist here.*

It's possible, even likely, that I'm hopelessly marooned here, and I'll be stuck inside this cube until the bliss of insanity claims me.

I watch as another vein inside the blue sphere winks out. My body is going fast.

Are Ash and Stefan still alive? If they can wake up my body, I'll be released from this cube. I can't dragon shift or time jump right now. To do those things, I have to be conscious and rested.

It sucks being a genie, waiting for someone to open the bottle.

## Smiles Are Good for the Soul

### ASH KINLEY

I SIT WITH MY BACK to the rock face behind our improvised campsite. A cold breeze blows, and beneath the smoke I smell the fir needles and the rotting leaves of late fall.

Tyler lies beside me, his breathing steady but shallow. I'm so worried about him. He probably saved our lives when he pulled us from Mahna's clutches, but he's paid a heavy price. I wish I knew what to do for him.

I hear a sound on the slope below me and raise my rifle. Thank God, it's only Stefan. I lower the rifle and exhale. He joins me, looking exhausted.

"Stefan, are you okay?"

He gestures for me to lower my voice and responds quietly. "Just need some food and sleep."

He looks like he has more to say, so I encourage him. "What is it?"

He puts the canteen and water-filled condoms on a flat rock, and the filter back in Tyler's pouch. "Redbeard is full-grown, so we're probably in the present. Our names aren't scratched in the bark, so this is a present where we don't exist."

I grimace. Somehow, being in the Stone Age seemed better.

Stefan continues. "And that's not all. I found tracks. Small. Not quite human."

Sun Walker flashes into my mind. "Gríma had some sort of witch with her, small, not human. She was dressed all in black, including gloves and a veil, and she had the ability to disappear."

Stefan narrows his eyes. "Disappear? How exactly? Did she become invisible, or did she go somewhere?"

"I think she went somewhere."

Stefan nods. "If she's a witch, she can probably travel into Som. It's a shadow plane where everything moves slower. But as far as I know, witches can't time travel, so I doubt those tracks are hers."

"I sure hope not. She creeped the hell out of me."

Stefan starts rummaging through Tyler's pouch. "It'll be dark soon. We should eat. We need our strength."

"Yeah, I'm starving. But what are we going to do about the tracks?"

"Normally, I'd want to do more scouting. But we don't have enough people. Best to lie low until Tyler wakes up."

We set up the small propane stove and use the filtered water to make green tea and a dinner of freeze-dried chicken and mashed potatoes.

Fortunately, Tyler's amazing pouch has a complete collection of aluminum camping dishes. After we eat, we'll have to clean them in a stream.

The mashed potatoes are shockingly delicious. Maybe it's just because I'm so hungry.

As Stefan eats, the color returns to his face. I watch his eyes reflect the setting sun. For some reason, despite the horrible circumstances, I'm so happy to be here with him. It's not just his strength, his experience, or his confidence. There's the deep connection between us that goes all the way back to our mated wolves.

As darkness falls, Stefan lights the pit fire. He makes some more tea, this time over the fire, to help preserve the gas for the stove. He cools the tea down with cold water and gives it to Tyler. It's messy, but a lot of the tea gets into him.

Stefan protects people, but he's also a nurturing person. Magnus was a great protector, but not a nurturer. He was always in need, always taking. A boy, not a man. Immediately I feel guilty for that thought. Poor Magnus is dead. I should do a better job of honoring his memory.

Watching Stefan, I try to imagine what he must be thinking right now. His entire town is gone, along with his parents and everyone he grew up with.

He sits beside the fire, and I move over next to him. "I'm really sorry about Corby."

He nods. "Me too."

"I'm sure we'll get it straightened out, once Tyler wakes up."

"Yeah, about that …"

Stefan removes a pill bottle from Tyler's pouch. "This is modafinil. It's a stimulant sometimes used by the military.

If Tyler doesn't wake up, I'm thinking we should try it on him. We could dissolve it in his tea."

I suddenly realize that Stefan has probably taken some of these pills. It would explain his rapid recovery from the jump.

I watch Tyler, his chest rising and falling with shallow breaths. Knowing him, he'd tell us to use the drug.

I nod toward Stefan. "I don't want to make things worse, but if he's not awake by morning, let's do it."

Stefan returns my nod and puts the pills in his pouch. "If we can't wake him up, we'll need to build a permanent hidden shelter. Somewhere near water, but on rocky ground where we won't leave tracks."

"Sounds good. I can hunt small game with my slingshot. Guns make too much noise."

"Good thinking." He pulls the inflatable mattresses out of Tyler's pouch. "Let's get bedded down for the night."

Stefan blows air into one mattress, and I inflate the other.

We lift Tyler's body onto one of the mattresses, though I doubt he can feel the difference right now. I just don't want him lying all night on the bare ground.

Stefan sets up the other mattress nearby. "You and I will have to share this one."

*Did he really just say that?*

Stefan senses the awkwardness. "Sorry, I mean we'll alternate. One person on watch and one sleeping."

I grin sheepishly. "Of course."

Stefan smiles. It's the first time he's smiled since we landed here. I know we're in a bad situation, where lightness doesn't come easy, but smiles are good for the soul.

"Stefan, do you mind taking the first watch? I know it's early, but I want to sleep now. I need to try something."

"No problem. Try what?"

I dig the space blanket out of Tyler's pouch. "I want to find our wolves."

He nods nonchalantly, but I see a spark of hope in his eyes.

I kiss him on the cheek, then curl up on the mattress and cover myself with the stiff, crinkly blanket. Tyler, being a dracoform, doesn't need blankets to keep warm. I don't get cold either, thanks to Seeker's gift, but the blanket gives me peace of mind.

# Quick Three Beers

## STEFAN HILDEBRAND

Hours later, staring out over a forest cloaked in darkness, I can't help thinking about that kiss on the cheek. It was nice, but it caught me off guard.

If I had to guess what it meant, I'd say it means she wants more, but knows this isn't the right time or place. She's right, of course. I feel the same way.

I shake off the speculation. I'm on watch. I have a job to do.

I feel a growing sense of unease, like I'm missing something. A bird chirps somewhere in the distance. I think I heard it earlier. I recognize the call. It's an olive-sided flycatcher. It has one of the more distinctive birdsongs. Every kid from Corby knows it. It's supposed to sound like someone whistling the words "quick-three-beers," but I've never heard it that way.

I know what's bothering me. I've never heard them singing this late at night unless there's a full moon. The sky tonight is cloudy.

Is it a *person* imitating the flycatcher? If so, the imitation is masterful. Why would someone do that? Is it a signal? Are there forces in the woods moving against us?

That doesn't make sense. Why would they give themselves away like that? Anyone who can do a call that well knows it would be out of place right now. Maybe it's intentional, a person who wants to be noticed. Or maybe it's a warning to me that something's wrong.

Or maybe I'm getting all worked up by some poor flycatcher confused by the smoke.

If I had my wolf, I'd invoke and survey the woods with my heightened senses. As it is, I feel blind and vulnerable.

Following my instincts, I kick dirt over our tiny pit fire. I take Tyler's pouch and attach it to my belt, then lean down to wake up Ash.

I shake her but she doesn't stir.

Don't tell me I've got *two* unconscious people to deal with!

I try to wake her again, shaking her hard, but she still doesn't budge.

I jump when Tyler suddenly mutters, "Rosemarie."

*Who the hell is Rosemarie?*

I hurry over and shake Tyler, but he remains unconscious. At least he's dreaming. I think that's a good sign.

The name "Rosemarie" seems to echo through the shadows, and I'm worried that our position's been compromised.

This is bad. I can't carry both of them. Not without invoking.

I crouch behind a boulder and watch the woods through the rifle scope. It's not a night scope, so I can't see much, but I do catch a hint of movement. There's something out there!

A sudden noise shatters the night. The banging of aluminum. I used some of Tyler's fishing line to string up a noisemaker made of camp dishes.

A gunshot cracks and the bullet chips the boulder only inches from my head! Who in the hell is shooting at me?

I return fire, taking my best guess at the enemy's location. I'm rewarded with a grunt of pain. Either I hit the bastard, or he wants me to think so.

I yell to Ash, but she doesn't wake up. What happened to her?

# VOICE ON THE WIND

## ASH KINLEY

ONCE AGAIN, I find myself in a white dress, standing on glowing blue ice. The clouds above shroud a sunless sky.

The land of Bright Ice is exactly as I remember. I still don't understand exactly *where* it is. Seeker once said it exists on the border between Niflheim, the world of ice, and Jotunheim, the world of giants. That doesn't help me much.

The wind whips up a tornado of frost crystals, casting sparkling light across the frozen vista. As before, I believe I'm here in spirit, not in body.

The wind carries something to my ear. I struggle to hear a distant voice calling my name. I can't tell the direction. The voice sounds female, weak and flat.

Is that Seeker? If so, why can't I hear her inside my head? The vargr speak mind to mind.

I continue to listen, but the voice falls silent.

I walk forward, wind whipping my red hair and blasting away the fog of my breath.

In the distance, I see the faint outline of the bone forest, though its sad song has yet to reach me.

A cloud of steam rises from the ice ahead. It's the hot spring where I first met Seeker. But there's no sign of the ice vargr.

I call out across the frozen expanse, using her full name, "She Who Finds Paths to New Lands!" The name comes out as music.

The wind drowns my voice. I feel alone and insignificant in this icy world. Did I really hear a voice on the wind, or was it my imagination?

When I was here last, the vargr had lost their connection with humans, lost their joy of living, and had fled to the dream burrows to die.

With the real world now devoid of humans, I wonder if the vargr have once again chosen that strange form of mass suicide. There's only one way to find out.

Ignoring the nervous flutter in my gut, I head straight toward the bone forest. Long before I reach it, I hear its sad song blowing through the skeletal branches.

As I get closer, the pale trees rise above the glow of the ice, and the sad, wordless song brings tears to my eyes.

To reach the dream burrows, I must cross this grim forest. I find myself running, in a rush to get it over with.

Bone limbs brush me as I pass. With each touch I sense the grief of the people trapped here. One woman lost her toddler to an illness. A young man's bride was murdered by bandits. A deaf girl's beloved dog was killed by a bear.

All these people are imprisoned here, trapped forever in their anguish. Why? Surely, they don't deserve it. If this forest was made of wood, I'd burn it down.

After what seems like an eternity, I burst from the bone forest, running full tilt. Feeling enormous relief, I study the frozen river before me.

This is the place where Seeker and I were attacked by giants. The hideous creatures wore patchwork clothes made of vargr fur and carried clubs made of bone tree limbs. Thankfully, there's no sign of them now.

Just as I remember, the ice is thin here, and I can see the dark water rushing beneath it. I ease out on my belly and roll across the ice. I'm careful to keep moving and spread out my weight.

The ice cracks but it doesn't break, and in a few minutes, I'm safely across and back on my feet.

As I continue my trek, the blue ice beneath my feet becomes patchy, revealing occasional glimpses of bare, smooth rock. The world grows darker as the glowing ice thins.

After a long walk, I see a cliff looming before me, wide enough to cover the entire horizon. As I get closer, I can make out the many fissures in the base of the cliff. Those are the dream burrows.

Last time I was here, I saw red light shining from the fissures. Seeker told me it was the glowing worms that consumed the flesh of the dead vargr.

This time, there's no such light. The fissures are dark.

I feel a spark of hope. Maybe the vargr haven't killed themselves!

I run to one of the fissures and step inside. Up close, they're bigger than they look, about five feet across. There's only a small patch of blue ice inside the burrow, so the light is faint. I squint for a better look and see a distressing sight.

It's the bones of a big vargr. But the bones are spectral, almost crystalline, as if they've been leeched of their whiteness.

Dozens of finger-length crimson worms lie dead around the bones. I'm guessing they consumed their only food source and then starved to death.

Swallowing a lump in my throat, I dart out of the fissure and check the others. It's the same everywhere. Dozens of vargr remains, probably hundreds of years old.

Having died in Midgard, they came to Bright Ice for their second life, and then threw it away, likely overcome by despair.

I wonder which bones are Seeker's. It's impossible to tell. I feel like I should bury them or something. But there are too many, I have no tools, and the ground is hard as rock.

Tears flood my eyes as I sit down against what was once a massive block of ice, its edges now rounded by the wind. Is this some sort of tribute marker? A collective headstone for these poor dead vargr?

Suddenly, I hear a male voice in my head. It sounds familiar. "Ash?"

I leap up from the block of ice and form a response in my head. "Who are you?"

When he speaks his name, it sounds like music, more feelings than words. I'd say it translates to something like "clever defender of the endangered."

"Can I call you Defender?"

"If you like."

"Where are you, Defender?"

"In the ice."

I circle the big block of ice and see the face of a gray vargr inside, lifeless as a bug in amber.

I press my hand against the ice, only inches from his frozen nose. "I think I know you. We spoke once. You're Seeker's mate, right?"

"I am."

*And you're Stefan's wolf!*

"Defender, are you alive in there? Can I get you out somehow?"

"I can only be freed by She Who Finds Paths to New Lands."

"What happened to you?"

"The dark elves killed us and slaughtered our children."

"I'm so sorry. We killed Gríma. I thought you were safe."

"The Svartr are only minions of the Dökkálfar. No one is safe while the dark elves live. They killed all the vargr, and my mate guided the slain to this place, to begin their second lives."

"But they killed themselves. Why?"

"For a time, our people found humans in Midgard to embody. Through them, we could experience life in the green forests of our former world. But quickly, the Svartr and dark elves took over, killing most of the humans and enslaving the survivors. The joy of walking the earth was forever lost. Rather than live out this dreary existence, our people chose to die in the dream burrows. All but me and my mate. We chose to lock ourselves in the ice and wait."

"Wait for what?"

"For you. Though I had given up hope, She Who Finds Paths to New Lands believed you would return."

"Where is she?"

"In the ice. Not far from here. She frees herself as we speak."

"How do I get you out of there?"

"She controls the ice. She will free me."

Feeling warm air on the back of my neck, I spin to see Seeker's toothy jaws only inches from my face. She licks my nose.

"Hello, Ash."

I throw my arms around her neck. Her white fur is dripping wet.

"Seeker! I missed you so much. How did you know I was coming?"

"After the dark elves killed our family, my spirit fell into a foul darkness, and I lost the will to live. Then the goddess Skadi came to me, told me how you had fought for us, and that you would one day return."

"Skadi's here?"

"I'm sorry, no. The Old Gods died long ago."

Ice cracks behind me. I turn to Defender breaking out of his half-melted cage. He shakes himself, casting a shower of water droplets.

For some reason, both vargr have that puppy smell, as if they've been newly born.

I give Seeker another squeeze. "I just knew you were alive. When I first got here, I heard your voice on the wind, calling my name."

Seeker cocks her head in puzzlement. "That wasn't me, child."

"But I heard a female voice ..."

Suddenly, the ice makes another cracking noise. Wait, no, it's not the ice!

What is that? It almost sounds like fireworks.

Another crack, even louder this time.

I look back and forth between Defender and Seeker. "Do you hear that?"

Defender cocks his ears. "I hear nothing."

# Eat the Svartr

## STEFAN HILDEBRAND

FRUSTRATED BY MY POOR NIGHT VISION, I grab the flashlight out of Tyler's pouch. It will no doubt draw fire, so I turn it on and set it on a rock about five feet from my position.

The brightness is shocking. Reminds me of the sun guns that KoR uses against vampires.

Looking downslope in the new light, I see people moving between the trees. I count three tall women, all wearing black body armor. They have small round mirrors hanging from their necks. The women all carry assault rifles outfitted with bayonets. And they all have big amber eyes.

Svartr!

The dark Were suddenly invoke and charge with incredible speed.

Because of their armor, I'll need head shots to take them down, something difficult in these conditions. Two of the Svartr are already airborne in high arcing leaps that will bring them down on top of me.

I opt to fire my assault rifle at the third Svartr, still on the ground. It's an easier shot, and I suspect that's their ranking soldier. My first bullet catches her in the cheek, killing her wolf. The second bullet catches her in the forehead, dropping her dead.

I roll to the side, holding my rifle up as a shield. The leaping Svartr land nearby, jostling each other in a frenzied competition to make the kill. I shoot one in the throat before the other is on me.

A bayonet grazes my ribs and pins my fur tunic to the ground.

The frenzied Svartr, fangs dripping, pins my rifle against my chest with her foot. Then she reaches down to gouge out my eyes with her black claws.

I try to reach my Glock, but it's pinned under my rifle. The Svartr's strength is at least triple my own. I'm going to lose this fight.

Suddenly, my opponent stops, her claws only inches from my face. She looks confused. Her body stiffens as veins of blue fracture her amber eyes. Her wolf leaves her as the skin on her face turns blue. She topples like a statue, revealing someone behind her.

It's a Were, this one with long white ears, electric-blue eyes, and long ice-blue claws dripping with blood.

The flashlight, though not pointed at the Were, casts enough peripheral light to make out her face. It's Ash! She's managed to reconnect with her wolf.

I sit up, freeing myself from the bayonet. The second Svartr, the one I shot in the throat, lies on the ground, seemingly frozen, with a slash across her blue cheek.

Ash crouches before me, her voice rough. "Are you okay?"

"I'm fine. What did you do to them?"

"I froze their blood. I mean, Seeker froze their blood. Can't say I feel bad about it."

"Do you see any more out there?"

She switches off the flashlight, awkwardly because of her long claws, and peers over the boulder at the forest below.

She sniffs the air as her bright blue eyes scan the shadows. "I think we're alone here."

I exhale in relief and climb to my feet.

Ash suddenly hugs me.

"I'm okay, Ash. Really."

"No, it's not that. I have your wolf. Can you feel him?"

My mind reels. "I don't feel anything."

"Give it a minute. I'm not as good at this as Cain. Just close your eyes and try to invoke. Your wolf's name is Defender. Well, that's a nickname really. He's Seeker's mate. He wants to help you."

"Defender? I've heard his name in my head, but I've never been able to pronounce it, or translate it. How did you get *Defender?*"

"Wish I could say, but I don't know. Try to invoke him."

Ash recovered our wolves once before, so I have no doubt she can do it again. I close my eyes and try to invoke.

Nothing happens. But I do feel a presence, familiar, but also different. This is a new timeline and Defender is not the same vargr he was before.

Rather than trying to pull him in, I relax and invite him to take the initiative. He steps in through the open door, and suddenly the dark forest around us comes to life.

The smell of the smoke is nearly overpowering, but under it I can recognize dozens of other scents. The Svartr, the trees and bushes, the moss on the rock face, the musky soil turned up by the fight.

As Ash continues to hug me, I hear the beating of our two hearts, and they begin to fall in sync.

I've successfully invoked. My wolf is back. I blink away tears, not realizing how much I've missed him.

At the sound of movement, Ash and I break our hug.

We turn to find Tyler lying on the mattress, his arm moving as if reaching for something in a dream.

We both rush over to him. Ash whispers comforting words in his ear while I check him for injuries.

"He wasn't hurt in the fight with the Svartr, but we need to move him. It isn't safe here now."

Ash nods. "Invoked, it won't be hard for us to carry him."

Ash, unaccustomed to her claws, uninvokes to make it easier to pack up the camp.

I check the bodies of the dead Svartr. All of them have a strange round mirror hanging from their neck. Are they for casting signals?

Sitting down on a boulder, I uninvoke and cradle one of their assault rifles in my lap and examine it. I'm awestruck.

The metal is a green-colored composite, very light, and I'm willing to bet rustproof. It looks a little like the assault rifle we brought here with us, only improved again and again, for dozens of generations. There are several switches on the weapon that I don't understand.

Somehow, the Svartr have developed superior weaponry. But their tactics suck. If these three had been smarter, they could have killed us. If there are more of them out there, I hope they're just as untrained.

I take their three rifles, along with the spare ammo. They also carry wicked daggers made of the same green metal. I stuff it all into Tyler's pouch, which amazingly, still isn't filled to capacity.

I also strip the body armor off the fallen Svartr. It's too big for Ash, but I put it all in the pouch. I think I can modify it later, but for now we have to get out of here.

My body stiffens as I hear the bird call again. Very close this time.

Ash doesn't seem to notice the sound, but she responds to my body language. "What's wrong?"

I shrug. "Not sure. Find cover."

We invoke and Ash joins me behind a rock.

In the darkness below, I make out a shape standing at the edge of the tree line. I call out to it. "Show yourself. We won't attack you."

A solitary man steps out of the gloom. He has the brown skin and strong cheekbones of a Native American. His head is bald, save for a short braid on the top, dyed bright red. It's hard to tell, but I'd guess he's in his midforties. He

wears a buckskin tunic and leggings, with greased mocca-
sins. In his hand he carries a thick fighting spear tipped by
a sharpened antler. At his hip hangs a metal dagger exactly
like the Svartr were carrying.

He speaks with an accent, but I understand him.

"I am Thayendanegea, of the Kanienkahagen, known
to your people as the Mohawk. You have no time to eat
these Svartr. Others are coming. Many others. You must
come with me."

He turns and walks back into the trees.

*Eat the Svartr? What the hell?*

Ash touches my arm, her face confused. "I wonder what
language he's speaking. I don't recognize it."

I realize that Ash couldn't understand his words, so I
take a moment to explain. "Before we met up in Norway, a
witch named Gudrun gave me the gift of tongues. It allows
me to understand, and be understood by anyone. Like a
universal translator."

Ash nods. "That's great! Eric had that."

"The man down there is Mohawk. His name is Thayen …
something. He warned us there's no time to eat the Svartr,
because more are coming. He wants us to follow him."

"He's a cannibal?"

"Maybe so."

Ash frowns. "We'd have to carry Tyler. Will Thayen get
freaked out if we're invoked, maybe try to eat us?"

"No idea."

Ash peers out into the shadowy forest. "He's close. We
can still catch him. Your call."

I answer without hesitating. "I think we should risk it."

The entire camp has been packed up into Tyler's pouch, which now hangs at my waist. I invoke and lift Tyler into my arms. Now that I have the added strength of Defender, it's like carrying a child.

As Ash and I hurry to catch up with Thayen, we see a disturbing sight. The ground on the slope shifts, as if a sinkhole is forming.

Neither of us wants to stick around and see what this is. We circle around the developing hole and run toward Thayen.

# JOYRIDING

## TYLER BUCK

I SIT INSIDE the cube, with nothing better to do than stare at the colored spheres and wait for my body to die.

Why aren't Ash and Stefan doing something to wake me up? Maybe they are, and I'm already too far gone.

Am I condemned to an eternity in this genie bottle?

I close my eyes and my mind wanders, drifting slowly into sleep.

ONE YEAR EARLIER

A green dragonfly zips past our pleasure barge as we drift at anchor in the middle of the Nile. Golden light bathes my bare chest as the sun sets behind the Great Pyramids. We are thousands of years in the past, and the pyramids are still faced with polished white limestone.

My queen reclines on a canopied throne at the center of the barge. She wears a translucent gown sewn with golden beads and held together by a thin belt.

I fan her with a palm frond, admiring her long blond hair and pale green eyes. Beneath the flimsy fabric of her gown, I see a few of her tattoos: an eagle, a horse, and a fish. There are many others, and I long to give each of them the lingering attention they deserve.

She and I are alone. She brought me on this barge for a reason, though her station forbids her from acting on her desires. Even as a slave, I must make the opening move.

I set aside the frond and kneel before her, dipping a linen cloth into a clay vessel filled with drinking water.

"My Queen, may I wash your feet?"

She scowls at me, her voice haughty. "Call me Pharaohess."

"I think you mean Pharaoh. There isn't a female version of that word."

She looks annoyed as I lift one of her ankles over my shoulder, rubbing the wet cloth down her leg and between her thighs.

"That is not my foot, peasant."

"I'm a slave, actually."

Rosemarie jumps to her feet, breaking character. "Gods, Tyler, you frustrate me! What does it matter what words we use? Why can't you simply enjoy it?"

"Sorry. Just want everything to be perfect."

She steps to the barge railing, running a hand through her hair. On her back, beneath the sheer fabric of her dress, I see a half dozen of the tribal tattoos that protect her. They look Celtic but they're actually from her Draig clan, part of the people the Romans called Picts. The tattoos are a little stretched and faded because she got them when she was young.

Rose stares out at the pyramids. "I'm sorry, it's not your fault. We should return to the Academy. I must study for an exam in my dimensional ecosystems class."

"I'm confused. You asked me to bring you here."

"Yes, because the anima is strong along the Nile. I hear the land sing and I want to stay. But we have little time left at the Academy and must learn what we can. We should not be out, as you have called it, joyriding."

I join her at the railing. "Let's stay a little longer. The pyramids are beautiful under the stars."

"You didn't bring me here for the scenery. You brought me here for strange Egyptian sex."

"I think you mean *freaky*."

"Is than an idiom?"

"Sort of."

She smiles. "Just once, I'd like you to *finish* washing my feet."

"I'll lick 'em clean right now."

I fall to my knees, chasing her bare feet with my forked tongue. She laughs and dances out of range.

"Do not make me laugh!"

I sigh, getting to my feet. "Okay, I'll do you a favor. No sex. But just give me thirty more minutes away from the Academy."

"I agree, but only if you explain how you're able to travel in and out of the Academy. We are supposed to be locked in, yes?"

"I do it by using anchors. Some people call them constructs."

She sighs. "I have not had that class."

"An anchor is an invisible mental creation built at a particular location. It's kind of like a homing beacon. It facilitates time jumps by allowing *temporadi* like us to travel in space as well as time."

"There is an anchor here in Ancient Egypt?"

I nod. "Specta Aeternal has an entire network of constructs, across the globe, and across all time periods."

"So why aren't other students sneaking out? You are the only one who can do it."

"The Academy and its surrounding area is shielded to prevent students from building anchors. Only Professor Southam has an anchor, and he keeps it locked. I suppose he thinks it's for our own good. I found a way to use it anyway."

Rosemarie nods, impatient. "How, exactly? Please teach me. I want to learn."

I hold up my hands. "I don't know how I do it. I just … can."

"Why do you torture me, Tyler? You must give me *details!*" Her raised voice attracts the attention of two children watching goats graze along the shore.

Rosemarie is passionate about things. Too passionate sometimes. She blames her Draigish blood. Though it gets us in trouble, I love that about her.

I grab the rope and haul the heavy anchor up from the muddy river bottom. "They noticed us. We should go. I'll explain it better when we get back."

Rosemarie nods, exasperated. Without thinking, she tears off her belt and lets her dress fall to the deck. Her pink nipples stiffen in the breeze as she walks to the canopy and puts her school clothes back on. I glance down at my jutting loincloth. She forgets what the sight of her body does to me.

The barge drifts north and around a curve in the river. I find my clothes and get dressed as Rosemarie waits on the throne. Damn if she doesn't look like she was born to sit on it.

I reach out and take her hand for the jump. Moments later, we're standing in the mango grove on the south end of Collegium Chronos.

Beyond the unbreakable glass barrier that marks the edge of campus, I see a stegosaurus munching on giant ferns.

The Time Academy was built in the late Jurassic period, long before the rise of humans. It makes sense. The dinosaurs are going to get wiped out anyway, so if a student does something to screw up this time period, it hardly matters.

Having the Academy in the distant past also solves another problem. If the timeline is fouled, the school is somewhat protected from becoming nonexistent.

I hug Rosemarie and whisper in her ear. "You're going to pass the test. I'll help you study. After the test, we'll talk about anchors."

She kisses me on the mouth, her lips gentle, her frustration gone. "Thank you."

PRESENT DAY

I emerge from the dream, still feeling Rose's lips on mine. But it wasn't a dream. It was a memory. Depression washes over me as I find myself back in my cube, sitting in one of the hardwood chairs. I miss Rosemarie. Random memories of her are filling the void here.

But maybe they're not random. Maybe this memory was a message from my subconscious.

If my body ever recovers, I'll be able to jump to the anchor at the SA field office in Quito, Ecuador. But there's a problem. I'm pretty sure that office doesn't exist in this timeline. Otherwise I'd have been greeted by the SA bureau chief when I hit the cube.

But what if I could use the anchor at the Time Academy? It wasn't built by SA; it was built by Professor Southam.

Southam has a fascinating history. He was born in Ancient Rome, where he served as a scholar. He used his time travel ability to help found the Academy. To date, he is the only known temporadi, or time traveler, who is also a dimensional traveler, meaning he can travel between alternate timelines. His hobby is collecting English histories from dozens of timelines. He's even adopted an English persona; handy, since English is now the universal language of time travelers.

Unlike myself, Professor Southam's birth in the Roman Era predates the fouling of this timeline. So, in all likelihood, the Academy still exists, Southam is still teaching, and he's built an anchor there.

I don't exist in this timeline. So, if I suddenly showed up there, he'd have no idea who I am. That shouldn't be a problem. I know enough about him to convince him that I'm his student. He'll have no qualms about setting me up with a metaphysician to heal the damage I received in the bad jump.

The big question is this: even if I wake up, will I be strong enough for a jump all the way back to the Jurassic? Can I even reach the Academy?

I lean toward the low table and examine the crystal spheres that monitor my health.

The green sphere, representing my soul, is still three-quarters dark. The red sphere, my mind, is completely lit. The blue sphere is about eighty-percent dark, meaning my body will die soon.

Fuck me. If that happens, I'll be trapped in here forever. How long before I become a raving loon?

# Waking the Dead

## ASH KINLEY

AFTER WE FOLLOW Thayen through the dark forest for nearly an hour, our Mohawk guide suddenly stops and turns to us.

He speaks. I don't understand him, but Stefan translates. "He says we shouldn't enter his camp in our wolf forms. Some of his people may become violent."

I nod and uninvoke. Stefan also uninvokes, and immediately I see the strain on him from carrying Tyler.

Thayen speaks again and Stefan translates.

"He's asking us if we have any mirrors. Mirrors are forbidden in his camp."

"I don't have any. Do you?"

Stefan shakes his head.

*That's a weird rule.* "Ask him why they're forbidden."

Stefan exchanges more words, and I can see him frowning. I don't understand most of what they're saying, but I do hear the word *Gríma*. I doubt this is going to be good news.

Stefan turns back to me, redistributing Tyler's weight. "Gríma is the mirror goddess. She can see out of any mirror, and even speak to people, mesmerizing them. We need to avoid any reflective surface, including still water."

"But we *killed* Gríma."

"I told him that, but he says we're wrong."

I frown. *Gríma is a goddess now? Impossible. Tyler torched her.*

Thayen continues forward, making a soft bird call, and in a few minutes, we arrive at a small clearing.

This seems to be a camp, but there's no light here. Uninvoked, it's hard to see anything.

Suddenly, a small group of Native Americans surrounds us. They carry spears, but they aren't pointed at us. I don't feel threatened, so I leave the rifle slung over my shoulder.

Thayen speaks to them, and then to Stefan. They talk for a long while, then Stefan sets Tyler gently on the ground.

The Mohawks surrounding us withdraw and there's a flurry of activity. They appear to be breaking camp. I see bloody human bones around a dead campfire. These people are definitely cannibals.

Stefan steps over to me and speaks quietly. "As far as I can tell, Columbus never came to the New World. But the Svartr and dark elves did, and only recently. The only white people here are the slaves the Svartr brought with them. When Thayen found us, he and his men were out looking for a group of escaped slaves. The Mohawk have a kind of underground railroad, getting escaped slaves across Lake Champlain, where it's supposed to be safer. Thayen thinks we're slaves who are also Were, like the Svartr. They've never seen that, and he wants to help us. I'm not sure why."

Thayen approaches and offers me a waterskin. He smells musky. My hand brushes his as I nod my thanks and take the skin. An oily residue on his hand rubs off on me. It's definitely the source of the musky smell. He didn't smell that way before. Did he just apply something to his body, possibly to mask his scent?

I turn to Stefan as he also accepts a waterskin. "Can you ask Thayen about the smoke? Also, why are they in such a hurry? Are we being followed?"

As Stefan and Thayen talk, I take a sip of the water. It has a leathery taste but is otherwise fine. We could probably use it to make some tea for Tyler, and give him the stimulant drug that Stefan found.

After a time, Stefan returns from talking to Thayen. His voice is soft, as if a threat lurks in the surrounding darkness.

"Thayen says the dark elves are building workshops under the mountains, turning them into volcanoes. The smoke is slowly killing the plant life and driving away the animals."

I nod silently, sensing Stefan has worse news to deliver.

"The dark elves are working with the Svartr, but the dark elves are the dominant partners. They're led by someone named Sindri. He rules a city called Dragonworks, located under Mount Mansfield."

"Why's it called Dragonworks?"

"Thayen doesn't know. But he does know there's a lot of slaves there, many on the verge of revolt. We may be able to use that somehow. Groups of dark elf hunters have been coming out of Dragonworks to search this area. At first, Thayen thought they were chasing escaped slaves, but now he thinks the dark elves were expecting us. They attack from below, which is why we saw that hole opening near our camp. The dark elf hunters have guns, and they also have something that Thayen called *clockwork hounds*."

"You mean like, robot dogs?"

Stefan stares out into the gloom. "Yeah, I think so."

"Damn. Something tells me my dog-taming powers won't work on robot dogs. We should wake up Tyler. Right now."

Stefan nods. "I agree."

Stefan pulls the pill bottle from Tyler's pouch. He takes two of the pills, crushes them between a pair of small stones, and pours the powder into his waterskin. After shaking the skin, he kneels and gives Tyler the water.

Thayen approaches and exchanges firm words with Stefan, then steps away to speak to his men.

I crouch down next to Stefan. "What's going on?"

"Thayen says we should abandon Tyler because he's as good as dead. I told him we won't do that. Thayen's pissed."

Worried, I massage Tyler's hands and legs, trying to squeeze some life into him. I whisper to Stefan. "How long for the pills to kick in?"

"Hard to say. Powdered, and on an empty stomach, maybe twenty minutes. But he's not exactly a normal human. We may need a bigger dose."

While we wait for Tyler to revive, Stefan uses the time to pull the Svartr body armor out of the pouch and outfit himself.

I rise and begin pacing. *If the pills don't work, we'll need a backup plan. Our Mohawk guide won't be sticking around much longer.*

Stefan approaches and starts hanging armor on my body. It's all too big, and it shifts around when I walk, but it's better than nothing.

He frowns at his work, clearly unhappy. "When we can build a fire, I'll reshape some of those pieces. But I really need tools to do it properly."

"It's fine, Stefan, thank you."

Thayen steps over to speak with Stefan, his voice grim.

Stefan turns to me. "They're leaving."

I glance at Tyler, who still lies motionless on the ground. It's been at least twenty minutes. He might need another dose, but I'm worried it could kill him.

I turn to Stefan, trying to keep the desperation out of my voice. "Before Thayen goes, ask him if he has something to write with, like some chalk or something."

Stefan looks puzzled, but he passes on my message.

Thayen shakes his head and leaves, followed by his other men. In moments, we've been abandoned in the woods. My eyes have now adjusted to the darkness, and I can see the simple shelters the Mohawks made from branches and boughs. All of them are empty.

I lean down and shake Tyler, speaking into his ear as loud as I dare. "Wake up, Tyler!"

Stefan studies me. "Why did you want chalk?"

"I want to make a shrine to Skadi. She's supposed to be dead, but I'm not convinced. In Bright Ice, I heard a voice that wasn't Seeker's. If Skadi is still alive, maybe she can help us."

Stefan nods. "Good thinking, but I don't think we have anything you can use as a marker."

"Give me one of those nasty knives you got off the Svartr."

Stefan's face tightens. He understands my plan and isn't happy about it, but he hands over the knife as asked.

I find a nearby boulder, sit before it, and cut the palm of my left hand. The knife is so sharp, the wound barely hurts.

Using the fingers of my right hand, I begin to draw on the boulder with my own blood. From my memory of Skadi's shrine, I draw a crude outline of a female archer on skis.

In the distance behind us, I hear a sound that makes my gut clench: the bark of an angry dog. The bark sounds mechanical, like a recording. Must be a clockwork hound!

I toss my rifle to Stefan, who stands guard over Tyler as I lean forward and press my lips to the makeshift shrine. Kissing the shrine was the way I entered Skadi's world once before. At the time, there was a risk. If I didn't have the *heart of a huntress*, my lips would get stuck to the stone. I sure hope that doesn't happen now.

As I kiss the cold boulder, I close my eyes and picture Skadi swishing down a hill on her enormous wooden skis.

Nothing happens.

The clockwork hound begins to bay, the mechanical howl close enough to feel in my bones.

I try to turn toward Stefan, but I can't. My lips are stuck to the stone!

# Buried with the Beast

### Stefan Hildebrand

Now that the Mohawks have abandoned us, there's no need to hide my wolf. The forest comes alive as I invoke, and I smell a heady rush of woodland scents.

I see the clockwork hound on a dead run, dodging trees as it charges our position. It looks like a huge pit bull that's been skinned alive and painted with molten brass. Its eyes are glowing coals. Steam pours from its mouth. As its legs move, I hear pistons pumping.

The good news is there's only one hound, and there's no sign of any Svartr or dark elves. Maybe this hound got out ahead of them.

It's up to me to stop the creature. Tyler is still unconscious, and Ash is in some sort of reverie, kissing her homemade shrine.

I take a knee for a better trajectory and fire three rounds from the assault rifle.

The first round hits the hound's curved head and ricochets. The second bullet misses. The third hits the hound's right front leg and the mechanical beast tumbles, cart-wheeling to rest at my feet.

I try to squeeze off a fourth round, but the rifle jams.

As I attempt to clear the jam, the hound lurches at me, tottering on three legs. The creature is too slow. Invoked, I easily step around, avoiding its menacing bite. I grab it by a back leg, swing it high in the air, and smash its head on a rock. Its skull snaps off and steam jets from its neck like a broken pipe.

The decapitated head, jaws snapping in slow motion, rolls like a bowling ball, coming to a stop where Tyler was lying. Except Tyler isn't there anymore!

The hound's head suddenly drops into a widening hole in the ground, a hole that must have sucked Tyler in. I can't let the dark elves get him!

Without thinking, I leap straight into the hole. I've now cleared the jam from my rifle and I'm ready to shoot these dark elf bastards.

I skid down a sharp incline, coming to rest inside what must be a tunnel.

It's too dark to see, even with my wolf vision. That often happens when I'm underground.

Somewhere ahead, I hear strange squeaking noises. The sounds are high-pitched. I wouldn't have noticed them if I wasn't invoked. There's also a strong, spicy scent in the air.

Annoyed by the darkness, I reach into Tyler's pouch, still at my waist. I pull out his insanely bright flashlight and turn it on.

I tense at the sight before me.

A trio of small, nude women, covered in mud, drag Tyler's unconscious body deeper into the tunnel.

But they're not human women, they're female elves. Their dark hair hangs in thick braids. They have pointed ears and angular faces. Their huge amber eyes squint against the bright light as they squeal in pain, turning their faces away.

The elf closest to me raises a green metal rifle and fires. She misses. I doubt she can even see me.

Holding the flashlight in my mouth, I swing up my assault rifle and shoot her in the chest. She makes a high-pitched scream, showing her sharp teeth, and then collapses.

The others, still shrieking in pain from exposure to the bright light, disappear into thin air.

I take a moment to assess the situation. The elves had no problem with killing me, but they were trying to take Tyler alive. Why?

I jump as something brushes my foot. The head of the clockwork hound lies at my feet, its jaws chomping in slow motion. I smash it with the butt of my rifle until it stops moving.

I've got to get Tyler out of here. I rush over and kneel beside him, giving him a quick once-over with the flashlight. He doesn't seem to be injured.

As I lift him over my shoulder, the ground shudders. The earth around the exit hole collapses, sealing us underground. How long before the entire tunnel gives way?

I put Tyler down, yelling up at Ash as I dig the dirt away with my Were claws. I hope she's able to help me. If we dig from both sides, Tyler and I might just get out of here before the whole thing collapses.

As I dig, I notice that the soil beneath my claws is oddly warm.

Suddenly, I hear a grunting noise behind me. Is Tyler awake? I turn around and shine the flashlight on him.

Tyler lies where I left him, but now he's shifting slightly, as if starting to regain consciousness. Standing above him is a clockwork bear, four times the size of the hound!

Steam drifts from the creature's ears as it sniffs Tyler's face. One bite from those massive jaws and Tyler will die.

Holding the flashlight in my mouth, I lift the assault rifle and fire. A shot to the head might deflect, as it did with the hound, so I aim for its leg, firing two quick rounds. The bullets ricochet, narrowly missing Tyler.

The bear snaps up his metallic head and roars like a jet engine. A shower of dirt rains down from the roof of the unstable tunnel. Will Tyler and I be buried with the beast?

The bear steps over Tyler and heads for me, taking its time.

It's clear now that I can't hurt the bear with my rifle, and if I keep trying, I could kill Tyler.

I yell at Tyler to wake up, and risk a glance behind me. There's still a lot of dirt blocking the hole, and no sign of help from Ash.

The bear continues to approach. Its huge body fills the tunnel and there's no room to maneuver or retreat. I hear gears whirring inside it as it shuffles toward me. Its burning coal eyes fix on me, anticipating the first bite.

I drop my rifle and jam my hand into Tyler's pouch, trying to find one of the green metal rifles I took from the Svartr. I still don't understand how they work, but now seems like a good time to learn.

The bear opens its jaws, impossibly wide, and I feel a cloud of hot steam on my face. It smells like burning oil.

Those jaws are powerful. I'm wearing body armor, but I don't expect it to save me.

# Gate Stones

## ASH KINLEY

As the clockwork hound approaches, I try to call out to Stefan, but my lips are sealed to the rock shrine. If I try to move, I'll rip my lips off.

What if I invoke? Can Seeker save me? I have to try.

I invoke as Stefan fires the rifle. I can't see what's happening, but I'm guessing the clockwork hound is attacking.

As Seeker enters my body, the black forest lights up as if illuminated by a full moon. The smells of the forest hit me: the sour smoke, the fir needles, my blood painted on the makeshift shrine.

I try to pull away from the rock, but even invoked, my lips are still stuck!

I feel helpless and vulnerable and push away a wave of panic. There must be *something* I can do.

I can't speak, so I scream out in my mind. *Skadi! It's me, Ash. I need your help!*

I hear a loud crashing noise as Stefan battles the hound. I still can't see what's happening, but I hope Stefan's winning.

Suddenly, the landscape around me changes. The shrine disappears and it's daylight now. I'm standing on the side of a snow-covered mountain!

I recognize this place. It's where I first met Skadi.

But she isn't here.

I call out to her, my breath fogging in the cold air, but she doesn't answer.

Where is she?

I take a moment to survey the terrain. Far below, at the bottom of the mountain, I see something covered with snow. Is it a cabin, or maybe a lodge? There's no smoke rising from it, so it's likely abandoned. Still, it's my only lead. I need to check it out.

I try to hurry down the mountain, but it's difficult without skis or snowshoes. My feet keep breaking through the crusty surface of the snow.

I resist the urge to panic and run. Yes, I need to get back and help Stefan. But last time I was here, only seconds passed in the real world, so I should have some time.

After a minute of slogging through the snow, my frustration grows. Even though I'm still invoked, this is taking forever.

An idea hits me. Maybe I can slide down, like at a water park.

I lie on my back, feet pointed downhill, and give myself a push. Sure enough, I begin to slide.

Faster and faster, I slide down the hill, building up incredible speed. Too much speed. At this rate, I'll smash into the cabin when I reach the bottom. That is, if I don't hit a tree first.

I reach out with my claws to slow myself down, and end up spinning wildly out of control. I try to roll over on my stomach and dig in with my claws to brake, but I hit a steep drop on the slope, bounce hard, and begin tumbling down the mountain. It reminds me of my last trip here.

I should be getting banged up pretty bad, but Seeker protects me. I hit a patch of soft snow near the bottom and manage to stop before I hit the cabin.

I crawl, trying to get to my feet, but I'm so dizzy I have to flop down and wait a few seconds for the world to stop spinning.

I recover quickly, thanks to Seeker, and walk the remaining distance to the cabin.

I can see now that it's not a cabin. It's more of a Viking longhouse, like the ones I saw in medieval Norway, but much fancier. It's made of wood aged to a dull gray, and carved with runes and symbols I don't recognize.

I knock on a front door carved from a single piece of wood. The door rattles, loose in the frame.

"Skadi!"

No response. I hear nothing but wind snaking through the snowy trees.

I have a strong sense that something's wrong.

The door doesn't have a handle. I push, but it appears barred from the inside. I kick it and the door explodes inward, thudding onto the wooden floor inside. Yikes, I didn't mean to kick it that hard.

I step inside and see the place is a mess. Water has trickled down from holes in the roof, causing the wooden floor to warp and crack.

A huge pair of skis, twenty feet long, lies on the floor just inside the door. I can see small tooth marks on them. Some creature has been gnawing on the skis.

There's an empty hearth, and a table and chairs covered by a layer of frost.

It doesn't look like anyone has lived here in a long time.

As I step deeper inside, I hear growling and crying. I hurry through the empty house, looking for the source. At one point, my foot nearly breaks through the creaky floorboard, but I manage to keep my balance.

I finally realize the sound is coming from outside, behind the house. There's no back door, so I quickly retrace my steps, exit through the front door, and circle around the house. I pass a stack of firewood covered with black mold.

At the back of the house I see a sight that freezes my heart in horror.

Skadi, now an old woman, hangs naked in a tree, suspended by chains around her wrists. She's still twice my height, but her blond braids have turned to white, and her face is lined almost beyond recognition. She cries as a pair of wolves chew on her dangling legs. As they rip away strips of meat, Skadi's legs heal instantly, but the pain must be excruciating.

I scream in anger and disgust, charging the wolves. They take one look at my invoked form and take off running. I might be able to catch them, but I let them go. They were hungry and just doing what comes naturally.

I rush forward and throw my arms around Skadi's waist. "I'm so sorry. Are you okay?"

Skadi looks down at me, her old eyes wide in disbelief. She speaks in a hoarse, weak voice. "I had a dream about you. I was calling your name. Seems it wasn't a dream after all."

"I made a shrine, but my lips got stuck. It took a while to get through."

"I'm sorry. I was too weak to help you. I can't believe you got through on your own. What an amazing feat! No mortal has ever traveled through a shrine they made themselves."

"What happened, Skadi? How long have you been here? Who did this to you?"

"This was Loki's revenge for the help I gave you, and the other things I did to thwart his plans. He put me here before he died in Ragnarök, before all the Old Gods died. He wanted me to suffer. I've been here for a thousand years."

Tears flood my eyes as I consider the torture she's endured. "I have to get you out of those chains."

Her voice is heavy with sorrow, "There was a time I could have broken them myself, back when I had worshippers. But Loki and his minions killed them all, and so I became powerless. No god remains a god without followers."

I kneel before her, bowing my head. "You aren't powerless, Skadi. You have my faith. I will worship you. I swear it."

Suddenly, Skadi drops from the tree, her chains broken. The snow softens her fall, and I help her sit up.

"Will you dress me, Ash? Inside, I have garments in a chest of drawers. They're woven with magic, so they should still be intact. I'd also like some fir needle tea."

I nod as I help her to her feet. "Of course, anything you need."

She whispers in my ear, "Thank you for saving me. I owe you my life."

Skadi sips her tea as she sits before the blazing hearth. She stares at the fire as she strokes my hair. Although there's a chair beside her, I've chosen to sit on the floor before her.

"Are you hungry, Skadi? I can go hunting."

She shakes her head. "Thank you, Ash, but no. I sense your time is precious, so please tell me why you came."

I nod, taking a deep breath. "The world as I know it, the world you call Midgard, has been destroyed. Civilization is gone. The Corby Were are gone. Gríma and the dark elves destroyed it all. My friend Tyler, the only person who can take us into the past to fix this, is unconscious and probably dying. And even if he wakes up, I'm not sure *how* we'll fix this. Can you help us?"

Skadi smiles grimly. "You know what I like about you, Ash? You don't ask for small favors."

*Is she teasing me?* "Please tell me there's a way. I'll do anything."

Skadi drinks the rest of her tea and sets the wooden mug on the floor beside her chair. "There may be a way, but it's dangerous."

I sit up straight, my hands on her knees like an eager child. "Tell me, please."

She gently cups the side of my head. "Such a brave one, you are. Very well." She takes a deep, tired breath. "The first thing to understand is that going back in time and killing Gríma won't prevent this catastrophe. The true enemy is Sindri, the dark elf king. Even without the Svartr, he would have found a way to unleash Ragnarök and make himself a New God."

I frown. "This is my fault. I should have gone after Sindri when I was in Norway."

Skadi shakes her head, her white braids swaying. "Killing his body would not have helped. He has protections in place. You must kill his soul. If his eternal soul is destroyed, it will be as if he never existed. It's a cruel act, yes, but the only way to reverse the damage he's caused."

"How do I kill his soul?"

Skadi pauses, looking pained. "I know of only one way. You must travel to Eventide and steal the Devourer."

"Devourer?"

"On the surface, it appears as a jeweled skull. But in reality, it's a metaphysical monster that destroys a soul. If the skull touches Sindri's blood, it will devour his soul. Be certain it touches no one's blood but his, or they will perish in his place."

"I'll be careful. How do I get to Eventide?"

"Fetch me the gate stones." She points to a box on the mantel above the hearth. For some reason, I didn't notice the box before.

As I retrieve the box, I feel objects shift inside. I hand it to Skadi. She sets the box in her lap and flips open the wooden lid.

Inside I see a set of runestones, not unlike others I saw in Norway. But I have a feeling these stones are special.

Skadi fingers through the stones, selecting some of them to spell out a word on the inside of the box lid. "This spells *Helheim*. Memorize the order of these stones."

ᚺᛖᛚᚺᛃᛗ

I nod, suddenly nervous. I haven't had to memorize anything since I left high school.

I burn the letters into my brain. "Okay, I think I have it."

Skadi nods, removing the runestones and spelling out another word. "This is *Midgard*. Memorize this as well."

ᛗᛁᛗᚷᚠᚱᛗ

I take a deep breath, calming myself as I study the letters. *I hope there aren't going to be any more of these.*

After another minute, I nod at Skadi. "Got it."

She puts the stones away and hands me the box. "When you are ready to travel to Helheim, spell out its name, arranging the stones in a clockwise circle. Step into the circle to travel to that world. After you step out of the circle, be sure to pick up the stones."

"Can my friends step through the circle too?"

Skadi nods.

"Okay, so when I want to come back, I spell out *Midgard?*"

"Exactly. The gate stones are simple. You don't need to be a *völva* to use them. Once you reach Helheim, travel toward the dark place on the horizon, where the un-sun shrouds Eventide in perpetual shadow."

"What is Helheim like? Are there people there? Are they dangerous?"

"Helheim is the land of the dead, a place that exists outside of time. Some of what you will see are illusions created by your own memories. But much of it is real. The dead you will encounter may appear to be alive, living or working in places they once frequented. Some may be old friends, now become enemies, and some may be old enemies, now become friends."

Skadi reaches for her cup and takes a sip of tea. Cool trick, considering the cup was empty before.

I'm eager to learn more about Helheim, and fill her silence with a question. "Why do people go to Helheim when they die?"

"Not everyone goes. Only those who still have lessons to learn."

"Can you tell me more about Eventide?"

"It's not fully bound in Helheim. It's more of a fringe city. The stronghold is ruled by Aud. He may actually be gone now, I don't know if he survived Ragnarök. I know little about Aud, save that he's a bastard godling of Nótt, goddess of night. Aud holds the Devourer as a prize in his collection of artifacts. He will not surrender it willingly. You must steal it and use it on Sindri. Once the Devourer tastes Sindri's blood, it will consume his soul, then the Devourer itself will die, its purpose served."

"Where does Aud keep the Devourer?"

"I don't know. I'm sorry, Ash, that world is closed to me. Once you are there, I cannot assist you."

I open my mouth to speak, but Skadi raises a hand to silence me. "Our time grows short. I have one more gift for you. One you might find ... distasteful. But you must not shy away. Do you understand?"

I nod, nervous. "I understand."

I grimace as Skadi bites off a small piece of her tongue and drops it into her hand. Blood trickles down her lower lip as she extends the hand to me. "Eat this, and in a few hours you will have the gift of tongues."

The gift of tongues! Like Stefan, Tyler, and Eric all have. That's something I desperately need.

I smile, though I'm feeling sick. "You're very generous, Skadi. Thank you."

My hand trembles as I take the small lump of flesh from her palm. Closing my eyes, I try to swallow it all down without tasting it. My stomach flips and I press my hands to my mouth, worried I'll throw up.

Suddenly, I cry out in pain. My left lower leg feels like it's burning! What's happening? Is this a side effect of Skadi's gift?

Skadi leans forward and kisses my forehead. "You must return now, brave girl. Events in Midgard have overtaken us."

She starts to fade away, but I have one last question.

"Wait! Can you help me wake up Tyler?"

Skadi cocks her head, concentrating for a moment. "That won't be necessary. It seems your plan is succeeding. When you speak to him, warn him that he will need his dragon to survive."

Skadi disappears, but I hear her voice. "Remember this. Helheim is a place within you. Each person must travel it alone."

*What does that mean?*

I don't have a chance to ask her.

I'm back in the real world, my lips pressed to the stone shrine. I'm clutching the box of gate stones and my leg hurts like crazy.

I pull my face away from the stone to find a limping, headless clockwork hound pawing my leg. Steam billows from the neck of the headless beast, scalding my skin.

I jerk my leg from its reach. A quick glance around shows no sign of Stefan or Tyler. What happened to them?

## LAND OF THE FREE

### STEFAN HILDEBRAND

I SHOVE THE GREEN METAL RIFLE into the mouth of the clockwork bear. The gun's bayonet sparks as it scrapes the animal's metallic throat.

I pull the trigger, but the rifle doesn't fire.

The bear reaches up with a steel paw, batting the barrel aside so he can get a clean bite at me. I use the momentum of his blow to pivot the stock around into the side of the beast's head. One of his steaming ears breaks off. The maneuver causes the flashlight to fall from my mouth. I really need three hands for this sort of work.

The strobe of the spinning flashlight distracts the bear for a second. I take that opportunity to examine my rifle. There are four switches on the weapon and I don't know what any of them do. So I flip them all and raise the weapon to fire.

This time, something weird happens. When I point the rifle at the bear, I get a physical sense of something pushing back on the stock. It must be a target sensor, physically telling me when the aim is true.

I pull the trigger again and the rifle fires full auto into the bear's face. I watch in amazement as layers of metal peel away from the creature's roaring head. Its massive jaws, full of razor teeth, shatter like broken glass, and its burning eyes turn into empty pits. Its head disintegrates under the withering fire, and the bear's neck spews steam toward the roof of the tunnel. As I shoot out the legs of the creature, my clip runs dry.

I pull extra ammo out of Tyler's pouch, in the form of preloaded clips. I figure out how to change the clip, surprised that the gun isn't even hot.

The clockwork bear, no longer a threat, shudders and grinds in a heap at my feet. Without the help of this captured rifle, I think the bear would have killed me and my wolf.

Suddenly, I feel a familiar warmth on the back of my head. It's the feeling I get when I invoke my wolf, but I'm *already invoked.*

I've had ghosts try to get into my head before, and it felt exactly like this. Are there ghosts here? Wait, no, I understand now.

During training with the Knights of Rome, we learned that Fae could use glamour to make humans see or hear things that aren't there, or feel emotions engineered by the Fae. Glamour affects the mind directly, much like a ghostly intrusion. Some glamoured emotions can be powerful enough to cause heart failure, or even suicide. KoR personnel investigating Fae were required to wear iron headbands to help ward off these illusions. But I don't need one. I'm Were, and I can fight it off on my own.

I check on Tyler. He's twitching a little. He might wake up soon, but for now, he's still out of it.

Calling out for Ash, I set down the rifle and start using my claws to dig out the collapsed tunnel entrance.

I can still feel the dark elves trying to get into my head. How long before they mount another physical assault?

Suddenly, there's a faint chemical odor, like a sweet bleach. It's subtle, and I doubt I would have noticed it without my wolf's nose.

Is it coming from the dead bear?

Drowsiness hits me, like I've been shot by a tranquilizer dart. My body moves slowly, as if caught in a giant spiderweb.

The dark elves are using knockout gas! The bastards are relentless.

As I look deeper into the tunnel, I see a shaft of light. Has the tunnel collapsed? Is that a way out? If so, it's probably safe there. The dark elves are afraid of light.

I stumble toward the light, feeling that something's wrong.

Wait, it's night outside! How could there be light shining down?

It's the glamour! The gas has weakened my defenses. The dark elves are luring me into a trap.

I step back, my body weaving, and manage to recover the flashlight from the tunnel floor. I shine the light ahead and hear more pained squeals, but I don't actually see the elves. Their glamour may be hiding them.

I realize I'm on my knees, and I don't remember how I got here. The cavern ahead seems to blur and spin. I'll be unconscious soon.

Suddenly, something grabs my arm, but I'm too drugged to fight it off.

I feel cool air on the back of my head and look around to see Ash in her wolf form, pulling me from the tunnel. She's talking, but her words sound muddled in my ears.

Once out in the fresh air, my head begins to clear. Ash goes back inside and emerges with Tyler, then she makes a third trip for the rifles and flashlight I dropped inside. The gas doesn't seem to be affecting her.

My head now clear, I take the green metal rifle from Ash and put the flashlight in Tyler's pouch. Ash slings our original assault rifle over her shoulder.

She hugs me intensely. "Are you okay?"

I nod. "I am, thanks to you. They gassed me, but my head's clear now. We should get the hell out of here."

Ash nods, using her wolf's strength to toss Tyler over her shoulder. "I got him. Lead the way."

I scan the shrouded forest with my wolf's eyes. We need to find a place with rock beneath our feet, so maybe the damned elves can't dig under us. I spot a hill not far from here, and there's no trees on top. That could be a good place.

I set a fast pace and Ash falls in behind me. I could probably carry Tyler now, but there's no sense pushing it. Ash is right to take charge of him.

Funny thing, if she wasn't Were, KoR would love her. She's the sort of dedicated fighter they want in their ranks.

Moving fast in our Were forms, we cross the forest with ease and climb the nearby hill. As hoped, we discover that the summit is solid rock. Let's see the elves tunnel up through this.

I turn to Ash. "It'll be light soon. Let's stop here and assess."

Ash nods and sets Tyler gently to the ground. "I still have Thayen's waterskin. I'll see if I can get Tyler to drink. He was moving a little. I think he's coming out of it."

We both uninvoke. As Ash tends to Tyler, I take some time to study the green metal rifle that saved me from the clockwork bear.

I sight the weapon on a porcupine sitting in a tree at the bottom of the hill. I flip the switches on the gun until I feel the target sensor kick in, pressing the stock into my shoulder. But nothing happens if I aim at a tree or rock. Is the sensor focused on living things? Does that mean the mechanical bear was alive in some sense?

I point the barrel downward, experimenting with the other three switches. One of them moves the trigger slightly forward, and I confirm that it's locked. That's the safety. A third switch has two positions, one marked with a single dot and one with two dots. It was on the double dot when I fired at the bear, so this must be the auto/semiauto switch. I still don't know what the fourth switch does, but I'm already feeling more confident with this weapon.

I open the pouch and remove the second of the three Svartr rifles, then stow away Ash's old rifle. She needs to upgrade to fight these clockwork creatures, so I'll show her how to use the new guns. But first, I need to know what happened to her at the shrine.

Ash has managed to get some water into Tyler, and he's groaning softly. I think he'll be awake soon, but I doubt he'll be strong enough to time jump.

"Ash, were you able to contact Skadi?"

She nods, then explains the details of her trip into Skadi's realm, including her gift of tongues. I'm in awe of Ash. She has a goddess for an ally! If I had known Ash growing up, I never would have left Corby to go undercover with KoR. She's the kind of woman you don't walk away from.

Despite the good news about Skadi, I have concerns about this mission to Helheim to steal the Devourer. "Ash, did Skadi say anything about Sindri or Gríma's influence in Helheim? Any chance they'll be waiting for us there, or that they'll chase us there?"

Ash shakes her head. "She didn't say anything about that."

"Okay, so Helheim is the land of the dead. What about Mahna? I'm pretty sure she's dead. What if she tries to grab me again?"

Ash's eyes tense. "I'm sorry, Skadi didn't say anything about that. But she did say one weird thing. Helheim is a place within you. Each person must travel it alone."

"Does that mean there won't be anyone there to interfere with the mission? Or does she mean we can't travel together?"

"I wish I knew. I could try to make another shrine, but it's risky. For a while, my lips stuck to the last one."

"Okay, don't do that. How's your hand?"

She holds up the palm she cut to paint her blood on the shrine. The wound is nearly healed already.

I whistle. "That's fast, even for a Were."

"I know. And the healing worked even when I lost Seeker. Same with my immunity to the cold."

"That shouldn't be possible. I wish Cain was here to explain it."

"Me too. We could use his wisdom about now. How do you want to handle this mess we're in?"

"The trip to Helheim sounds like our best shot. But even if we can steal this Devourer thing, we still have to infiltrate Dragonworks and kill Sindri. I have no idea how to do that."

Ash takes a long breath. "Let's keep our eyes open for opportunities. Skadi might find ways to help us. In any case, we can't go to Helheim until Tyler wakes up."

Both of us invoke as we hear a branch crack somewhere at the base of the hill. I adjust the switches on Ash's new rifle and hand it to her, whispering quickly. "It's set for full auto. Safety's off. Pull the trigger in short bursts."

She nods, and we crouch behind a boulder, aiming our weapons down the hill.

To our left, the sun rises, blood red in the smoky haze.

Below, I see a group of four people: three men and a woman. They're dressed in rags, covered in grime, and clearly exhausted. One of the men is older, with a gray beard, one man has stringy red hair, and the third man is bald and sickly thin. The woman has short dark hair and wild, searching eyes.

I whisper to Ash. "What do you bet it's those escaped slaves that Thayen was talking about? They're probably headed to these rocks for the same reason we came."

Ash nods. "We should uninvoke. We'll scare them."

I pause, scanning the area for other threats. I see nothing else but the porcupine. "Okay, let's uninvoke."

We drop our wolves and slowly stand.

Ash gives the group a friendly wave. They freeze, and for a moment I see terror on their smudged faces. But they relax after getting a good look at us.

I call out, gesturing for the slaves to approach, "Come on up. We won't hurt you."

They speak quietly among themselves. Uninvoked, I can't hear them. The oldest male in the group, a white-bearded man with a milky left eye, seems to be in charge. He calls to us, "We're coming up."

I whisper to Ash. "Can you understand them?"

She shakes her head. "Not all of it. Only the word *up*. Skadi said it would take a few hours for the gift to take effect. I need a little more time."

"Okay, then it's probably best for you not to talk. If they hear a foreign tongue, it might freak them out, and I want to see if they have any useful intelligence."

Ash nods, looking frustrated.

I put down my rifle and Ash does the same.

The slaves stop a short distance away, and the old man eyes me suspiciously. "Your clothes are strange. Who is your master? Where are you from?"

"We have no master. We're from a place far away."

"Does this place have a name?"

I think for a moment. "The Land of the Free."

The old man looks intrigued. "Where is this place?"

"Far, far away, I'm afraid. Farther than you could walk."

He looks suspicious now. "Why are you carrying fae-cast rifles?"

*So, these guns were made by the dark elves, not the Svartr. Interesting.* "We captured them from the Svartr. The weapons are new to us. What can you tell us about them?"

The old man spits. "The metal, *sindrion*, is evil. It can only be forged in shadow, and heals itself when damaged."

"But they're good weapons. We'll gladly trade you one for information."

He holds up his hand. "No. These are the masters' weapons. The guns will bring a curse on us."

"What do you mean? What kind of curse?"

"Bad things happen to slaves who touch the masters' guns. Illnesses, accidents, insanity."

*Is this just superstition? It would make sense that the masters would try to scare the slaves away from the guns.*

I need to know more about these people. "Who's your master?"

"Sindri. We serve him, *served* him, before we escaped from Dragonworks."

I nod. "Come sit down. We have food for you. Eat, and tell us about Dragonworks."

They shuffle forward. *Food* was the magic word. These poor people probably haven't eaten in days.

Ash and I exchange a look as the smell of them hits us. I'm not sure any of them has *ever* taken a shower or bath.

I can see Ash is frustrated at understanding only one side of the conversation, but I'll have to fill her in later. I don't want to spook these people by raising more questions about our origin.

The old man spots Tyler lying on the ground. "What's wrong with him?"

I shrug. "I'm not sure, but I think he'll wake up soon."

Ash and I break out Tyler's camping gear. We don't have enough water to cook the dehydrated food, but there's plenty of granola bars, mixed nuts, and crackers. The slave woman and the youngest man weep as they eat the food with shaking hands.

Ash's eyes tear up as she watches them. I wish I had her good heart, but I think I lost that long ago, working for KoR.

As the escapees eat, they tell us the story of Dragonworks. The underground city, run by Sindri, is dedicated to one mission: creating a clockwork dragon!

*Shit, that bear was bad enough. Think about fighting a dragon.*

I wonder if that's why they want Tyler alive. Maybe they need an actual dragon for their plans.

I question the old slave about the layout of the city, and the resistance movement that Thayen told us about.

The old man explains how Sindri is using a mining aqueduct to filter important minerals from the soil. Each day, the aqueduct is dammed and the filters scraped clean of the valuable minerals. The old man and his friends escaped during that time, sneaking out through the empty aqueduct.

The slaves involved in mining operations have it bad there, and all are loyal to the resistance. The only people more eager to rebel are the slaves who get fed to the dark elf young. Baby dark Fae start their lives in larval form and need human blood to grow.

The slaves have plenty of reasons to fight, but the resistance is still too weak and disorganized to mount a serious threat against Sindri. This particular group of slaves took the risk of escaping because they were tired of waiting for a rebellion that might never come. Now free of Dragonworks, they're making their way to the *bulging lake*, which I understand to be Lake Champlain. From there, the Mohawks will take them west, to an area where the dark elves have yet to build any workshops. The air there is clear and the game plentiful.

I see the old man is tiring, so I lean forward to ask the most important question I have. "We need to sneak into Dragonworks. What's the best way to do that?"

The old man laughs, then realizes I'm serious. "You don't look like slaves. They'll kill you before you get ten steps inside."

*I'm ready for that objection.* "Would you be willing to trade clothes with us and tell us how to get inside? We'll throw some food into the bargain."

The old man takes one look at his torn, filthy rags. "Done. I'll show you what you need to know."

We find a thin patch of soil atop the rock layer, and the old man draws two maps. One shows the position of Dragonworks in relation to Mount Mansfield. The second map shows the aqueduct and a little of the underground city near the mines. Being miners, these former slaves haven't been into the main city and can't tell me much about it.

However, there is a way in. The aqueduct they escaped from will also give us entry into the Dragonworks mines. We just have to hurry through the empty channel while they're scraping the filters. If we're too slow, we could drown when they turn the water back on.

Once inside, we'll have to avoid the Svartr guards and try to make contact with a human mining slave. The secret hand sign of the resistance is an index finger casually scratching the skin above the heart.

I thank the escaped slaves for their valuable information. They're eager to gather their promised food and get moving.

We give them all the remaining food that isn't freeze-dried. Ash, who doesn't know what's going on, looks surprised when we begin to exchange clothing, but she rolls with it. Stowing our body armor in Tyler's pouch, we strip down to our underwear and slide into the filthy slave rags. The clothes reek and they scratch my skin. The thin leather sandals feel like blister-making machines. But this will make an excellent disguise.

It would have been better to get these clothes *after* our trip to Helheim, but we may not get another opportunity like this one.

Ash and I also remove Tyler's clothes and hand them over to the slaves. His eyes open for a moment, but he doesn't seem to see us. I remove a fourth set of clothes and shoes from Tyler's pouch. Oddly, the slaves don't seem fazed that so much stuff has been removed from the same pouch.

As the slaves change into our clothes, I see that none of them are wearing underwear. It's clear their bodies have been abused by whips and hard labor. I hope they all make it across Lake Champlain. I'm sure they'd rather die than return to the mines.

Though we haven't exchanged names, there are handshakes all around as the escaped slaves depart. None of them ask why Ash never spoke.

After they leave, I explain everything to Ash, and together we get Tyler into his slave clothes.

To her credit, Ash doesn't complain about the downgraded clothes. She just seems excited about the prospect of taking out Sindri. The torture of Skadi really pissed her off.

As I survey our slave clothes, I realize there's a problem. They're full of holes and rips, revealing our underwear in many places.

Ash sees it too. "I'm guessing slaves don't wear underwear."

I nod. "I'm afraid it'll give us away."

Ash shrugs, pulling her bra and panties out from beneath her rags. I do the same with my boxer briefs.

Ash didn't blush or turn away. She has total confidence in her body. And she should. It's amazing.

She eyes me, worried. "Tyler and I are immune to the cold. But what about you?"

"I'll invoke if I get cold. If it gets really bad, I saw a coat with the camping gear."

Ash nods, then glances over at Tyler. "Help me with his undershorts?"

I nod. Ash invokes, lifting his body as I remove his briefs. *This feels ... weird.*

Tyler suddenly wakes up.

Of course, he would wake up *now*.

He blinks, groggy as he sees us take his underwear. His voice is barely audible. "Damn, you guys know how to party."

# Six O'Clock High

## TYLER BUCK

FEELING WEAK, I struggle to sit up. It's dawn and I'm in a forest. The sight of the red sun, along with the dirty rags I'm wearing, makes me feel like we've arrived in a postapocalyptic world.

The truth is, I don't care how bad this world is. Anything is better than that freaking crash cube.

I smile at Ash and Stefan. "Where are we?"

Ash crouches beside me with sympathetic eyes. *This isn't going to be good news.*

"We're in the present, not far from where Corby should be. But the town isn't there. In this timeline, the modern world never developed. None of us were ever born."

*That doesn't make sense.* "You're sure we're not in present-day Norway?"

Stefan nods. "Very sure."

My mind reels. I'm not surprised to find us on a rogue timeline. But how did we get from Norway to Corby? The mental anchor I built here to allow my return disappeared when the timeline got fouled. I shouldn't have been able to traverse the space between Norway and Corby. No one can do that without an anchor.

Ash shakes my arm. "Tyler, are you okay?"

I realize my eyes are closed and I've been drifting off into my thoughts. I need to focus.

"Sorry, I'm a little off. The jump went wrong. I need a metaphysician. There aren't any here, so when I get my strength, I have to jump back into the Time Academy."

Ash nods. "What can we do to help?"

"Nothing, Rose. I just need some food and a few days to rest."

Ash frowns. "Who's Rose?"

"What?"

"You just called me Rose. And you mentioned the name Rosemarie when you were out of it."

*Pull it together, Tyler.* "Sorry, I'm not myself. Rose is my girlfriend. We attended the Academy together. We're kind of, separated."

Stefan hands me my pouch. "We had to dig into your gear. Hope that's okay."

I nod, taking the pouch and letting it drop into my lap.

Stefan scratches the stubble on his cheek. "I gotta ask how it holds so much. Magic?"

I shake my head. "No. It's spatial engineering technology. From the future. We think it's powered by a tiny black hole."

Stefan's eyes widen. "Man, how did you get that?"

"About eighty years ago, people from the future visited the present, or what used to be the present. We call them the Magi. They left a number of gifts behind. Folded space was one of them. The pouch part is just cosmetic. We added that. You can also dress it up as a box, or even a pocket."

Ash's face brightens. "That's so cool! Why did they give it to us? What else did they bring?"

"No one knows why they did it. And I'm not supposed to talk about the other gifts."

*I'm off my game. I shouldn't have said anything about the Magi.*

I dig around in the pouch for a granola bar, but most of the food is gone.

"Somebody was hungry."

Stefan steps over. "Sorry about that. Give me the water filter, canteen, and a couple condoms. I'll get some water and we'll cook you up some freeze-dried food."

"You want my condoms?"

"Yeah, for extra water."

"You put water in them?"

Ash laughs and Stefan grins. I'm not sure why that's so funny, but I give Stefan what he asked for.

Stefan turns to Ash. "There's a stream not far from here. We passed it coming in. I'll be back soon. Can you fill Tyler in on what's happened?"

"Sure, but be careful."

"I will. And you keep an eye out downslope."

After Stefan leaves, Ash tells me the unbelievable story of what's happened since we arrived here. I can't believe I missed it.

Before she finishes, Stefan returns with the water. I give him my pouch and he removes the cooking gear and begins preparing a meal of chicken fajitas using what's left of the clean dishes. For some reason, the smell sickens me, but I don't say anything.

After Ash tells me about Skadi's plan to steal the Devourer from Helheim, Stefan asks a question.

"Tyler, what's your take on Mahna? Should I be worried about her in Helheim?"

I shake my head. "I'm not sure. She had your soul tethered, but I felt the bond break during the jump. Otherwise we wouldn't have made it here. I'm guessing she can't do anything to you remotely, but if you met in person again, who knows?"

Stefan looks pissed. "I'm kinda hoping I do meet her. Wouldn't mind killing her twice."

*It's time to give them the bad news.*

"Guys, I think we need to split up for a while. I'm in no shape for a trip to Helheim. I need to go to the Academy and get fixed up. I can't take you there. I'm not strong enough, and it's against the rules to bring in outsiders. You should make the trip to Helheim without me. Then when I'm better, I'll return from the Academy, and we can all go into Dragonworks together."

Stefan nods. "Okay, Tyler, but there's no way we're leaving you alone when you're not a hundred percent. We'll wait with you until you recover enough to jump to the Academy."

I force myself to stand, but I need Ash's help.

"I appreciate you both keeping me alive. But you won't be able to stay with me. The smell of that food is making me sick. I need to *feed*. I need to eat while in dragon form, something raw and alive."

Ash nods. "That makes sense. Skadi told me something about you. She said you'll need your dragon to survive."

I nod. "She's right. I think my body is still dying. I'll last longer as a dragon. And jumping is actually easier in dragon form. If I can feed, and rest up for a day or two, I can probably make the jump to the Academy. I'll get patched up there, then I'll return. Meet me here when you have the Devourer, then we'll take out Sindri together."

I take off my slave clothes, put them in my pouch, and hand the pouch to Stefan. "Hold on to my stuff. I can't use it as a dragon, and you may need it in Helheim."

Stefan nods and takes the pouch. "Thanks. We'll take good care of it."

I take a minute to explain the crash cube, and the importance of holding on to it. Both of them are amazed to hear that I've been in the cube the whole time.

Ash steadies me as I sway on my feet. I'm worried that I'll pass out again. I need to get moving. "Is there a wide-open space where I can shift?"

Stefan points to a flat area at the base of the hill, covered with patches of dirt and brown grass. "How about there?"

Feeling even weaker now, I stagger on my feet. "Can you help me get down there? I'll be fine once I shift."

They help me down the mountain, both averting their eyes from my dangly bits. Thankfully, I've never been shy about nudity. That comes in handy when you're a shifter.

As we arrive at the open space, Ash squeezes my arm. "I'm worried about this plan, Tyler. You're a big target, and they have guns. It'd be easy to pick you off from the ground."

"Yeah, I was thinking about that. Are there any large bodies of water around here?"

Stefan points opposite the rising sun. "Lake Champlain is about thirty miles west. In places, the lake is over ten miles wide."

Tyler nods. "That's perfect. I can spend my time out of sight, in the water, feeding on fish."

We say our goodbyes. I shake hands with Stefan, but Ash insists on a hug. I try to keep my eyes off her insanely revealing slave clothes. This would be an awkward time for an erection.

Stefan and Ash return to the base of the hill, giving me plenty of space to shift. I hope I have the strength for the transformation, it would suck if I failed in front of them. I can picture myself running naked, flapping my human arms in a futile attempt to fly. It makes me chuckle.

A wave of dizziness hits me. I stumble and nearly fall. I see Ash starting toward me, but I hold out a hand to stop her.

*I can do this.*

Shifting into a dragon, or back again, is enough to cure most physical injuries. I once survived a gunshot that way.

But right now, I'm suffering from a metaphysical injury. My soul is damaged and the transformation will do nothing to heal that. I just hope I can recover enough strength to make one jump to the Academy.

Shit, I nearly forgot I'll need an anchor to get back here. I seem to have made it here without an anchor, but that may be part of why I got hurt so bad. No sense making things harder.

Fortunately, these constructs have never been hard for me, and won't take much effort.

I focus my mind and imagine driving a crystal stake into the ground. The stake is engraved with the current date.

Of course, there's no real stake there, just an invisible mental construct. I visualize it as a crystal stake, but other temporadi imagine their own objects.

With the anchor in place, there's no sense in delaying the inevitable.

It takes a lot less effort to shift than I expected. Immediately, I feel the familiar burning sensation as my skin becomes transparent and splits open. My arms and legs lengthen, and my fingernails become long, crystal claws.

I also feel the flare of anger that marks a shift. At first, I thought dragons were just naturally grumpy, but I've heard this happens to a lot of Were when they shift, regardless of their animal.

I look down and see the crystal scales on my forelegs. Normally, they reflect rainbow light onto the ground, but the sun is too weak now to produce that effect.

I flick my long tongue to gather scent, then touch it to the roof of my mouth to taste it. The smoke is bitter, drowning out all other scents.

I'm still wearing the contact lenses that disguise my orange eyes as brown. I discovered long ago that I can leave them in while in dragon form, and it doesn't bother me. Of course, now, my flaming orange eyes are *huge*, and the contacts so small in comparison that they disappear into my pupils.

I turn my horned head toward my friends. I see more colors with my dragon eyes, and Ash's hair is many shades of red. Seeing me for the first time as a dragon, her eyes are wide with wonder, but Stefan looks his usual cool self.

I nod goodbye to them. I *can* speak in dragon form, but my voice comes out rumbling and threatening, so I don't use it much.

Now comes the tricky part. I stretch out my wings, run a few yards to build up speed, then flap madly to take off.

I'm relieved to find myself airborne before running out of space in the clearing.

I have to flap again, *hard*, to clear the trees. I barely make it. My claws brush the treetops as I pass.

There are no thermals here to ride up to altitude, and I'm too weak for a direct ascent. I'll have to risk a bit of exposure taking a diagonal path to elevation.

With the wind in my face, I'm feeling better. My belly roars, and I can already taste those fish I'm going to catch.

I look back toward Ash and Stefan, but they're hidden by the trees. Damn, I'm not climbing as fast as I'd like. I'd better feed soon. I need more gas in the tank.

After traveling several miles, I manage to gain a few thousand feet of altitude, but I still haven't climbed out of the smoke layer. The bad air is burning my lungs, and I'm not sure I can make the thirty miles to Lake Champlain without stopping to rest.

Suddenly, my sensitive ears pick up a shout, somewhere down on the ground.

Have I been spotted? Am I about to be fired at? At my current altitude, it would be a tough shot, but still doable.

I look down and see a group of people running through the trees and emerging into a boggy area, where they are slowed down. Thankfully, they're not looking up at me, so maybe I'm safe.

I notice the group is wearing our clothing. These must be the slaves we traded clothes with.

Behind them, darting fast through the trees, I see a large group of invoked Svartr chasing down the fleeing slaves.

Those poor people are making slow time in the bog. Even on stable ground, they'd have no chance of outrunning Were.

I see a few faecast guns among the Svartr. Attacking them would be a terrible risk.

Still, those poor slaves gave us important information about Dragonworks, and they sure don't deserve what the Svartr are about to do to them.

Intervening now, when I'm at less than half strength, would be the stupidest thing I've ever done. There's no way I'm gonna do that.

And yet, I'm already in a dive, swooping down on the Svartr from six o'clock high.

# Moonshine and Mind Games

## ASH KINLEY

I missed it when Tyler, in dragon form, attacked Gríma at the Jotunborg. Until today, I've never seen him as a dragon and feared I never would. I feel so honored to witness his amazing transformation.

As a child, I had a book about a dragon, and it was one of my favorites. Now I've seen one in real life. For me, the attraction of dragons isn't the teeth, claws and fire. I'm jealous of their ability to fly. As a girl, I sometimes dreamed about sprouting wings and flying away from our family farm.

After Tyler disappears over the treetops, Stefan and I get to work. It takes over an hour to prepare for our trip to Helheim. First, we clean the camp dishes in the nearby stream. Then we have to figure out a way to carry our pouches. The slave clothes don't have belts, so we cut up one of Tyler's wool sweaters, something we missed in the trade with the slaves, to make shoulder slings for our gear. I know that Tyler is immune to the cold, so the warm clothes in his pouch must be kept on hand for his travel companions, like Stefan and me.

Stefan is worried we'll get separated in Helheim, and he tries to give me the pouch with Tyler's gear. But I insist that Stefan keep the pouch. Tyler's crash cube and all our survival gear are in there. Carrying it is a huge responsibility, and I think it's safer with Stefan.

Both Stefan and I carry the faecast rifles, which come with handy sling straps so we can hang them over our shoulders. Stefan takes time out to explain in detail how the guns work, and to show me how to invoke without the claws on my trigger hand so the rifle is easier to use while in wolf form.

In addition to the rifle, I carry two pouches rigged to shoulder slings. The first is my leather ammo pouch, with the Wolf Head constellation. But I'm no longer carrying lead balls in there. Instead of slingshot ammo, it now holds the time compass and a pair of spare clips for my faecast rifle.

My second pouch, the one Sassa's village gave me, once carried my dead phone, but now holds Skadi's gate stones. I've taken them out of the wooden box to make them easier to carry. The box, my phone, my slingshot and its lead ammo, are all now stowed in Tyler's folded space pouch.

I'm not happy about trading my slingshot for the faecast rifle, but the clockwork animals are just too dangerous. Later, when we sneak into Dragonworks, I'll probably have to stow the rifle, but for now, I'm carrying it.

Even though I'm traveling light, this won't be a comfortable journey. The slave rags, seemingly made of burlap and fiberglass, stink and itch, and the leather sandals are making my feet sore. I wonder if Stefan's outfit is also bugging him. If so, he isn't complaining. Those poor slaves. I can't believe they had to wear this all the time.

Finally, we're both ready to go. We find a flat space in the clearing and I start arranging the gate stone runes in a clockwise pattern that spells Helheim in Norse.

Stefan checks the settings on his rifle. "I'd like to go through first. Follow me and retrieve the stones. What's the plan if we get separated?"

"Skadi said that Eventide is marked by a dark place on the horizon. I have no idea what it looks like, but it's shrouded in shadow, so it shouldn't be hard to find. If we get separated, we can meet up just outside of it."

Stefan nods in agreement as I finish laying out the stones.

I examine the circle once it's complete. There's nothing to indicate this is a magic portal to hell. I guess I was expecting something flashier, like red lights and a floating Satan head.

Stefan eyes the stones skeptically. "Is it working?"

"I hope so. Skadi says you just step into the circle."

Stefan takes a deep breath and his eyes find mine. "Okay, then, wish me luck."

Suddenly, we move forward into a kiss. I'm not sure who started it. It's not a *let's have sex* kiss, but more of an *I'm off to the war* kind of kiss. It's really great, and it's over too soon.

I look at Stefan to gauge his reaction, and see that my gaze is making him uncomfortable.

"Stefan, I have a better idea. Let's step into the circle together. I know you're worried there's something dangerous on the other side, but I'm more worried about being separated."

He mulls it over as he holds me in his arms. "Okay, but if we're going in together, let's do it right. Wrap your legs around me."

I laugh, happy to comply. I kiss him again as he carries me into the circle.

One moment, we're in the clearing, surrounded by forest, and the next I've fallen on my ass in the middle of Pennsylvania farming country. The sky is cloudy, and the low rolling hills are covered with brown vegetation. In the distance, a barn burns, sending a twisting snake of black smoke into the air.

As I feared, Stefan is nowhere to be seen. There's not a single person in sight. My jaw tightens as I get to my feet and readjust the rifle hanging on my shoulder. Wherever Stefan is, I hope he's safe.

It's too much of a coincidence that Helheim looks like where I grew up. Something tells me that hell is in the eye of the beholder, and Stefan is seeing something completely different from me.

I'm struck by a frightening thought. I'm not sure why it didn't occur to me before. Could my dead father be here? Will he be looking for me, seeking vengeance for the dog attack that took his life? After all, I trained the dogs that killed him, and I sicced them on him.

I take a deep breath to calm myself. I'm a grown woman now, and I'm too strong for him to hurt me anymore.

I check to make sure Seeker is still with me. She is! It's a relief to know I'll be able to invoke here.

I slowly turn, surveying the horizon. It's cloudy and I don't see any dark spots, but there is a place where the clouds are a little heavier. I'll head in that direction and hope I find Eventide. But before I leave, I gather up the circle of gate stones around me.

After traveling for about ten minutes, I see activity ahead in a field of dead corn. It's a group of Mennonites in wide-brimmed black hats, hunching as they pick corn and throw the black cobs into wheelbarrows.

The Mennonites I know, the Christian community who lived near us when I was growing up, are peaceful people. They shouldn't be dangerous. Maybe I should ask them how far it is to Eventide.

I call out a greeting, but they ignore me, their faces hidden by their hat brims.

I pass a barrow of cobs. They're covered with black mold and crawling with worms. I make a grunt of disgust, and one of the men suddenly looks up at me. He has no eyes, ears, nose, or mouth. His face is just a flat sheet of flesh.

I gasp, passing around him in a wide circle. One by one, they all look up at me, all of them without eyes, noses, or mouths. It makes me queasy.

What does this mean?

I jog past the cornfield and through a settlement of ram-shackle wooden houses. Ahead, I see a group of children with toothy grins, dancing around a pit of coals. Some sort of charred animal hangs on the spit over the coals. God, I hope that isn't a dog. I fight a strong urge to vomit. I hold my nose as I pass the kids. I don't want to smell the meat.

I think of my poor lost dogs, Shasta and Lucky, and pray that they're safe.

As I leave the settlement, I run into a Mennonite woman milking a black-and-white Holstein cow. Thank God, she has a face.

She smiles at me as her hands work the cow's udders, squeezing milk into a bucket. But it isn't milk, it's steaming squirts of yellow pus.

I lean against an old wooden fence and vomit.

If this world was built from my imagination, I've really outdone myself.

When I'm feeling better, I invoke and begin running. I need to get past all this craziness and find Eventide.

As I run, I stare at the brown grass on the ground ahead, trying to empty my mind. If this nightmare is coming from my own thoughts, I need to shut them off.

After what must be an hour, I uninvoke and stop to rest my sore feet. For the first time since I saw the cow, I look up and scan the horizon. I'm a little off course, but the dark clouds in the distance have gathered into a single point. I'm pretty sure that must mark Eventide.

The area around me looks familiar. I realize I'm standing next to Mr. McPhee's barn. In the next property over, I see my family home with its peeling mustard paint. Through one of the windows, I catch a glimpse of someone moving inside!

My heart pounds. Is my dead father in there? No, not my father, I have to stop calling him that. I'm a wereling and Neil Torp was my father. The man the dogs killed was just my abuser.

I feel a powerful urge to run. Even though I have a gun, and I have Seeker, part of me is afraid.

I don't want to be afraid anymore.

I march toward the house.

Doubts gnaw at me as I approach the front door of the run-down property. I reach the handle with shaking hands and find it locked. For some reason I wasn't expecting that.

Last time I visited home, the house had new owners. They told me Mom sold the house and left me a video, but it was destroyed before I could see it. Maybe the new owners are inside.

I knock on the door.

I cry out in shock when I see who answers.

It's Mom!

Her cheeks are gaunt and her skin sickly yellow. She's swaying on her feet, and her breath stinks of alcohol. As usual, she's drunk.

Her bloodshot eyes widen. "Oh Jesus, tell me you're not dead!"

I shake my head. "No, Mom, I'm not dead."

She steps up and hugs me fiercely. "Where have you been? I searched all over for you."

"It's a long story."

*Am I talking to a figment of my imagination, or is Mom really dead?*

She pulls me inside and closes the door. The air in the house is humid and smells like rotten eggs. "Mom, what's that stench?"

"Corn mash. I have my own still now, come look."

She pulls me toward the kitchen, but I resist.

"Where is your husband?"

"The dogs killed him, remember?"

I nod warily, following her into the kitchen.

Sure enough, she's set up a crude still to make moonshine, and there's a pot of boiling corn mash on the stove.

When I was little, we visited my uncle, and I remember he had a setup like this.

Mom lifts a jug from the counter, taking a long swig of moonshine. When she speaks, her voice is rough from the alcohol. "Want some?"

"Pass."

She stares appreciatively at the still. "So much stronger than the wine I used to drink. Don't know what I'd do without it. I'm happy now, maybe for the first time." She smiles, showing yellow and brown teeth.

*What's really going on here? If this is some sort of message from my subconscious, I don't get it.*

"I have to go, Mom."

I turn to leave but she snatches my arm with a bony hand, anxiety in her voice. "Wait, you just got here. We have to talk about the video."

I freeze in my tracks, then slowly turn to face her. "I never saw the video. It was destroyed."

She frowns. "Then you don't know?"

"Don't know what?"

She nibbles a bit of skin from her chapped lower lip. "Sit down, Ash."

"I'm fine standing. What was in the video?"

She stares at the floor. "When I was younger, I met a man named Neil Torp."

For some reason, I feel a flash of anger. "Yes, from Corby. I know he's my father. Is that what the video was about?"

She stares at me in shock. "How did you know?"

"It doesn't matter."

I turn again to leave but hear her calling after me. "Wait, there's more. Something happened *after* I made the video."

*I don't want to hear it, but something makes me stop.*

Mom continues, speaking to my back. "About a month after you ran away, the police were still looking for you and the dogs. The doctor told me I was dying. Bad liver. That's when I saw a way to protect you."

Filled with morbid curiosity, I turn to face her. "What did you do?"

"I confessed to killing your father. I mean, your stepfather. It was the only way to clear you."

*Maybe this isn't my imagination. I'm not sure I could make this up.*

"You're saying you went to jail?"

She shakes her head. "Prison hospital. And, Ash, I died there."

Even though this probably isn't real, a wave of guilt washes over me. I killed her husband and abandoned her with his body. If she really died, is some of the blame on me?

I feel myself trembling and resist a strong urge to invoke.

Mom takes a long swig from the jug, then wipes her mouth with the back of her hand. "I'm sorry, Ash. I was a terrible mother, too weak to protect you from him. I'm not asking for forgiveness or anything, I just want you to know you're safe from the police."

*There's no way this is my mom. The mother I knew wouldn't have apologized for failing me, and she sure as hell wouldn't have gone to jail for me. This is all moonshine and mind games.*

I march for the front door, but Mom staggers ahead of me, blocking the way.

"Come on, Ash, you came all this way to talk to me. Sit for a while, tell me how you got here."

I shake my head. "I didn't come here to talk to you. I'm trying to save Corby. I'm trying to save the world."

I push her aside and she tumbles to the floor.

I harden my heart, resisting the urge to help her up, and stalk out the door.

As I leave the farm, I glance back, relieved to see she isn't following me.

I set a course for the dark place on the horizon and continue my trek.

As I walk, Mom's words echo in my head.

I think I understand what's happening. I always wanted her to be a good mother, to love and protect me, to put my needs above her own. But she failed me every time.

Maybe the scene that just played out was scripted by my own imagination, custom-made to give me closure.

On the other hand, I've never heard of anyone going to hell to get closure. This is a place where people get punished for their sins. But this isn't hell, this is Helheim, the Norse version of hell. Maybe things work differently here.

None of this makes sense. Why would Mom end up in a Norse hell? She was Christian, in name if not in deed.

This must be all in my head.

I wonder if Stefan is going through something like this. So far, this place doesn't seem dangerous, but it can really mess with you.

I look up to the horizon to check my progress, and I'm surprised to see a huge dark area ahead. I'm very close now. That was fast. I guess hell must have run out of torments.

I scan the area, hoping to see Stefan, but there's nothing out here but low rolling hills filled with dead scrub and the occasional sickly tree.

I do notice one odd thing. Even though there's no sun overhead, I have a shadow now, and it stretches toward the dark area ahead.

Skadi said the horizon was dark because of the un-sun. With a normal sun, shadows stretch *away* from the light source, but this un-sun pulls them in.

As I continue forward, the land grows dark around me. When I look back, I can't see where I've come from.

In the gloom ahead, I spot a massive structure dominating a hill. It's a castle made of a glassy dark stone, maybe obsidian. The castle's high wall encircles the entire hill, and I see the tops of other buildings rising inside the wall. This isn't just a castle, it's a town, or a small city. It must be Eventide.

I stiffen as a movement catches me off guard. There's someone sitting under a dead tree about halfway to the castle. Is that Stefan?

I invoke for better vision. The figure stands. It's not Stefan; it looks like a woman in a long black robe, holding a book in her hand.

She's seen me, and she's walking toward me.

There's something familiar about her.

# SHE WITH THE WHITE WOLF

## STEFAN HILDEBRAND

I ARRIVE IN HELHEIM without Ash in my arms. Somehow, I knew that would happen. I'm worried about Ash being alone. I want to be there for her if something goes wrong.

I'm standing in a nightmare version of the forest outside of Corby. All the trees are fallen or sagging, suffering from rot.

I check to see if I can summon my wolf. I can. That's a relief. I need to stop calling him *my wolf*. Ash says his name is Defender, but that's going to take some getting used to.

I look on the ground and see the ring of gate stones around me. If Ash picks them up, then I'll know she's okay.

After a moment, the stones disappear one by one. I'm glad she's okay. Looks like we're each in our own version of Helheim.

Visibility is limited here, so I need to find a place where I can see the horizon and locate the dark place that marks Eventide. Climbing a tree isn't a good idea. Most of them look sickly and unstable.

As I move through the dead forest, I pass a deer drinking from a stream. As it turns to me, I see a terrible neck wound, crawling with maggots. The deer is dead. Its white eyes stare at me. Its mouth is red and I realize it's been drinking from a stream flowing with blood.

This can't be real. Ignoring the dead deer, I follow the blood upstream.

Faint screams blow in on a wet breeze. I invoke, picking up the pace. The smells here are disgusting. Nothing but death and decay.

The screams grow louder as I abandon the bloody stream and climb a nearby bluff.

From my vantage point, I see what looks like Corby, fully engulfed in flames. It's burning to the ground while its people scream in terror.

I know this can't be real. My people would not respond with such panic. But I should check it out just to be sure.

Still in wolf form, I run toward Corby, stopping to climb for another view when I can.

The problem is, no matter how far I run, Corby gets no closer. It's like one of those bad dreams where you run and run but don't go anywhere.

I'm convinced now it isn't real. It's just a distraction, meant to get under my skin. I decide to ignore it, and make my way toward the dark patch of clouds on the horizon. I want to get to Eventide before Ash and make sure it's not dangerous there. Of course, now that I think of it, there's no guarantee that Ash and I will arrive at the same version of Eventide.

I run through the forest for nearly an hour before I see something that makes me stop. There's a faint glow of warm light coming from the woods on my far right.

It's probably another distraction, but I should check it out.

Moving through the decaying forest, I find what looks like a sinkhole. The hole has smooth walls and is about five yards deep. At the bottom of the hole I see the waxy stubs of a few flickering candles, the source of the light.

At the base of the hole is an entrance to a cavern. Even more light streams out from the cavern.

My wolf nose catches a familiar, sweet scent, but I can't quite place it.

Something tells me I need to look in that cavern.

The wall of the hole is too slippery to climb, but in wolf form I could jump down easily, and jump back up when I wanted out.

This could be a dark elf trap, but I can't feel them in my mind, and I can't imagine them wanting to be around all this light.

I could jump down, get a glimpse of the cavern, and jump back up in mere seconds.

This may not be a good idea, but what the hell.

Rifle ready, I jump into the hole, landing lightly on the balls of my feet.

Looking into the cavern, I can't believe what I'm seeing!

Lying on a raw slab of stone is a sleeping girl surrounded by glowing candles. Her arms are crossed over her chest. I recognize her long blond braids and the freckles on her cheeks. It's Elin, a Sleeping Beauty around eighteen years old. The sweet smell is the vanilla perfume she wears.

I kind of expected to see Mahna here. Elin is a shock. She was my first love. I knew her growing up, and probably would have married her if Corby hadn't sent me undercover at KoR.

It occurs to me that Elin could be Mahna in disguise. I glance at my arm, where Mahna carved her name into me, but the wound has healed.

As I approach Elin, I don't feel that sense of wrongness, or sudden exhaustion that I felt when Mahna pretended to be Ash. Maybe this really is Elin.

We had plans to go off to college together. When that fell through, she couldn't handle being abandoned by me. A year after I left Corby, she invoked and ran into the woods, never to return. Word is she went feral, remaining in her wolf form for so long that she couldn't return to human form. Feral Were usually roam the wilderness for the rest of their lives, living like animals.

What happens now? Am I supposed to kiss Elin and wake her up? Then we'll swap stories about our lives since we broke up? Am I supposed to apologize for leaving her, for breaking the promises we made to each other?

There's no evidence that Elin actually died. She's missing, yes, but no one ever found her body. I don't think the girl before me is any more real than my vision of Corby burning. She's just a hallucination generated by my guilt.

Suddenly, Elin wakes up. Her head rolls toward me and her eyes focus, wide and unbelieving. "Stefan?"

She sits up on the rock slab, rubbing her eyes and looking at me again. A smile bursts on her face, and suddenly she's racing toward me, white gown flapping, braids trailing in the air. She has something in her hand, not a weapon, but more like a piece of jewelry.

She leaps into my arms, nearly bowling me over. Her eyes are warm but her skin is cold. Now that she's closer, I detect the sharp scent of silver mixed with her vanilla perfume.

As she withdraws her embrace, she wraps something around my neck, and I hear it click shut. Instantly, Defender leaves me.

Elin pulls a small key from the folds of her gown and swallows it with a triumphant smile.

I reach up and feel a silver torc locked around my neck. I pull but can't break it, not without the strength of my wolf. I realize now there's no way I'm getting back up out of the hole.

This *was* a trap. And a good one. My guilty feelings about Elin got in the way of my judgment. But if this is all in my imagination, how was I able to trick myself? Maybe this is more like a dream. I've had stuff like this happen in dreams.

I keep my face calm as I speak to Elin. "What do you want?"

Her voice shakes with anger. "For you to hear my story, you son of a bitch."

"I'm listening."

"Do you know what happened to me after you left?"

"They said you went feral."

"Do I seem like the type to lose my mind so easily?"

"No."

"Good, at least you can give me that. I didn't go feral. I went to visit the Norns in Trenson."

"Now we're back to crazy. Those werebears are dangerous."

"I know their reputation, but I needed their help."

"With what?"

Her voice rises sharply. "With *you*. What did you think? I was sad, Stefan. I lost interest in food, people, everything. I had nothing to lose at that point."

"Wish you hadn't gone there, Elin. The Norns don't help unless it's in their own interests."

"Yeah, I got that."

"So, what happened?"

"They didn't care about my pain. They only wanted to talk about you. They said you would have three loves, and I was only the first. Your third love would be the one that lasted. They didn't say her name. They called her *she with the white wolf.*"

I feel my skin prickle. *It's Ash!*

I force myself to calm down. I don't know if this conversation with Elin is real.

Elin crosses her arms, furious. "Why so quiet? Don't you want to know what happened next?"

I take a step back. "No."

"Well, I'm telling you anyway. They *killed me*, Stefan. They hacked me apart with axes. Then I'm guessing they ate me. Now I'm here, for eternity, without my wolf, without anyone."

*Sounds like something the Norns would do.*

Tears pour down her freckled cheeks. Illusion or not, I can't help pitying her.

"I'm sorry, Elin, I never meant for this to happen."

"Why did you leave me, Stefan?"

"I didn't want to. It wasn't easy. I chose duty over love."

"Yes, but *why?*"

I think about it for a moment. "Because duty benefits all of Corby. Love only benefits you and me."

She shakes her head sadly. "You don't get it, do you? Corby was built on relationships, on love. Without love, there is no community. Love is also a duty. You and your pig-headed father could never see that. But your mother saw it, didn't she? Did she ever divorce him?"

I nod.

"Good." She wrings her hands nervously. "I want to know something, Stefan, and you better tell me the truth. Have you met your third love yet?"

I frown. "There's no way in hell I'm having that conversation with you."

"If you want that silver collar off your neck, you'd better answer my question."

I feel a growing tension in my body. This confrontation feels pretty real. What if I'm actually trapped down here with my dead high school girlfriend?

Something tells me Elin can't handle the truth. I look her in the eye and speak with conviction, "No, I haven't met anyone with a white wolf."

Her body relaxes as she exhales in relief. "Good, then it's not too late for us."

"What do you mean?"

"We can still be together, here in my home."

"What home, Elin? This is a cavern with a slab of rock."

She laughs. "Oh, is that what you're seeing? Come on, you can do better than that."

She takes my hand, pulling me toward the rock slab. "Come to bed with me, Stefan, and I'll make you forget why you left me."

I pull my hand away. "Elin, I won't play this game with you."

She turns on me, almost snarling. "Yes, you will! You owe me that much."

"I won't. I'm sorry."

Her face turns cold. "I swallowed the key to your silver collar, and you can't escape the hole without invoking. You're trapped here, Stefan. The way I see it, you have two choices. You can stay with me and we'll make a life together, or you can tear my body apart, like you ripped my soul apart, and pull the key from my bloody guts. Which will it be?"

*One thing life has taught me, there's always a third choice.*

I reach into Tyler's pouch, rummaging around until I find a stirring spoon with his camping utensils.

Then I tackle Elin. My rifle and pouch slip from my shoulder and drop to the floor.

I pin her to the ground. "I'm sorry, Elin. I didn't want it to be this way."

She shrieks and gags as I force the spoon into her mouth and down her throat. Fortunately, it seems that the dead still have a gag reflex. After a minute of Elin's cursing, crying, and heaving, the small key finally comes up. I use it to unlock the silver collar.

Immediately, I invoke Defender.

I gather my things from the floor and step away from Elin, but she remains curled on the ground. She screams out between sobs. "I hate you!"

I shake my head. "Not as much as I hate myself."

Then I turn, walk out of the cavern, and leap up out of the hole.

Elin's crying fades behind me as I race through the dead forest, eager to leave my past behind.

I don't know for sure if she's really dead, but I have a hunch she is, and that what's happening is real. If the Norns killed Elin, they have a lot to answer for.

As I dart through the forest, I think back on the good times with Elin. That's the way I want to remember her, happy and smiling.

After a time, I realize I'm no longer in the forest. How long have I been running? I feel the familiar burning sensation, caused by being invoked for too long.

In the distance ahead, I see a city on a hill, protected by a high black wall. Inside the city, at the summit of the hill, stands a black castle. The entire area is cloaked with the darkness of night. I'm guessing this must be Eventide.

I walk a circuit around the hill, hoping to find Ash.

In moments, I spot her red hair, shining in the shadows. She's speaking to a tall woman in black robes, carrying a book. The tall woman is standing profile to me, so I can't get a look at her face.

Ash suddenly points her rifle at the woman. What's happening? Is Ash in trouble?

I sling my rifle off my shoulder and sprint toward them.

# Nÿrland

## TYLER BUCK

As I DIVE DOWN on the Svartr, I realize the conditions are perfect. The sun is obscured by clouds, so my dragon shadow won't give me away.

The invoked Svartr, all women dressed in buckskins, howl gleefully as they chase the slaves. By now, the Svartr could have easily shot them, but they haven't. Either they want them alive, or they want to kill them with tooth and claw, for sport.

The timing couldn't be better. I close in just as the Svartr emerge into the bogs. Without the cover of the trees, they're vulnerable to my dragon fire.

As the air rushes past, I flatten my dive to make a sweep over them. But there's a problem. The lead Svartr is too close to the slaves. If I roast her, I might hit the slaves as well.

There's a way to do this, but it could get messy. I know I shouldn't be taking this risk, but these Svartr are pissing me off.

As I fly past the rear Svartr, I spit a stream of liquid. It bursts into sticky orange flames upon contact with the air and splashes down like napalm on the line of Svartr.

My plan was to stop the fire stream before reaching the lead Svartr, but that happened anyway because I've run dry. Usually, I'm good for several blasts of fire before I need to regenerate my reserve. But today, one blast is all I get. The problem is I haven't fed, so I'm not at full strength.

The burning Svartr scream as their flesh melts. Their wolves can't save them from my fire. Dragon fire burns almost anything, and it can't be smothered or extinguished with water. Being covered in my liquid flame is a death sentence.

Rather than pulling up from the sweep, I dive toward the lead Svartr, now nearly on top of the slaves. Hearing the dying screams of her comrades, she spins just as I strike.

My timesight kicks in, and I see overlapping images of the Svartr. The darkest image is the Svartr's present position, and the brightest where the Svartr will be a second later.

When I was learning my dracoform powers, my sapphire mentor, Gammachu, taught me how to anticipate an enemy's moves. The timesight power works well against animals and normal people, but not as well against highly intuitive fighters.

The Svartr is going to get off a shot, but I'm at the end of a committed dive, so there's nothing I can do to stop her.

The Fae bullet sears into my right wing, shattering a support bone.

I grab the Svartr with both foreclaws. My right wing fails and I feel my left leg break as I crash into the bog. Water splashes around me as I curl into a ball and roll thirty yards, nearly crushing the escaping slaves.

The Svartr, still held in my foreclaws, is dazed but recovers quickly. I curl my body around her as she attacks with her claws, trying to reach my underbelly.

I bite her hard on the head. It should have been a lethal strike, but it only kills her wolf.

My timesight shows her about to scratch five bloody lines into my soft stomach scales. I allow it to happen and use the opportunity for a second bite, plucking her head from her neck.

The fight is over.

I lift myself onto three legs and survey the area. The slaves never stopped running, and now they're across the bog and into the trees. I hope they make it to where they're going.

I look back and see no sign of living Svartr. I killed them all, but I'm sure more will come.

Blood drips from my wing and stomach, and my broken leg throbs. I'm out of fire, I can't fly, and I can only limp on the ground. If I'm attacked now by more Svartr, I'll be killed.

Or would I?

Something's bothering me about this fight. That lead Svartr had me dead to rights, but chose to shoot my wing rather than my head. Sure, it may have been a bad shot, but I think they want me alive. Stefan told me how the dark elves tried to pull me down into the tunnel. It would have been easier to kill me. Do they want to question me? Do they think I have important information?

Maybe they want to know more about Specta Aeternal and our mission to protect the timeline. If they try to question me about that, they'll be disappointed. SA puts mental blocks on all its agents to protect those secrets.

I need a plan to deal with my immediate problem. I'm hurt, but there's a fix for that. Shifting back into human form takes very little energy, and the shift itself would heal my physical wounds. The problem is, I won't be able to return to dragon form without more rest, rest that my dying human body probably can't produce. If I shift to human form, I may get stuck there and die, or else be forced to attempt a jump to the Academy before I'm recovered. Jumping is easier in dragon form, so if I have to make an impossible jump, I should do it as a dragon.

I think the best thing to do is feed, then hide somewhere and rest up until I'm strong enough to jump. These physical injuries hurt, but they're not going to kill me. I can tolerate them for a day or two.

The problem is, in my current state, I'm in no condition to catch prey. There's only one solution.

The bog is too exposed, so I limp around, gathering the Svartr dead in my jaws, and I stack them in the cover of the forest. My broken leg throbs with pain, but I can't afford to be out in the open.

I squeeze my injured dragon body between two huge trees, then squat down to feed. Before eating each of the Svartr, I use my foreclaws to strip away their guns and the mirrors hanging around their necks. But I leave their buckskin clothes on; those don't bother me.

After gorging on a half dozen bodies, I feel the rush of a feeding high, and the pain in my body begins to dull.

Suddenly, I hear the voice of a woman calling my name. Is it Ash?

I scan the surrounding forest with my high-color dragon vision. There's no one here.

The voice calls out again, and I realize it's coming from the ground beneath me.

With great effort, I shuffle back and see a mirror resting on a bed of dead pine needles. But instead of seeing my own reflection, I see a face in the mirror. It looks like a Svartr with metallic features and a black mask around her eyes. Is that Gríma?

Her glowing red eyes are oddly calming.

She speaks to me through the mirror. "Hello, Tyler. It's been a long time."

*I remember now. Stefan and Ash warned me that Gríma could be in mirrors. But how is that possible? I killed her in the fight at the Jotunborg, over a thousand years ago.*

*Could this be dark elf glamour? I doubt it. I'd sense it if they tried to get in my head.*

Gríma speaks again, her voice sympathetic. "Are you hurt, Tyler?"

My dragon throat wasn't made for speaking. I have to concentrate to pronounce each word, and my voice comes out deep and rumbling.

"You can't be Gríma. She's dead."

She shakes her head. "I'm not Gríma, I am the goddess, *Mirror Gríma*. Tell me, Tyler, where are Ash and Stefan?"

Despite my hatred of Gríma, and my naturally angry dragon personality, I find myself warming to her and wanting to answer her question. "I don't know where they are. We split up."

"I see. Well, it doesn't matter. I'll find them eventually. But right now, I need your help."

"Why should I help you? Look what you've done to the world. The land is covered with smoke and the only humans are slaves. You've created a hell on earth."

"I'm not happy about the smoke, but Sindri is working on that. In a few years, his workshops will burn clean. As for the slaves, I consider that progress. If freed, they'd breed like insects and destroy the world. You've got it backward, Tyler. This isn't hell on earth. We're creating heaven on earth. We call it Nýrland, meaning *new land*. We're very proud of it, and you'll play an important role here."

As I listen to her words, they start to make sense to me. Maybe Gríma isn't as bad as I thought. I find myself growing dizzy and struggle to maintain the conversation. "What role will I play?"

Gríma smiles. "You're special, Tyler. Dragons are rare and beautiful creatures. Sindri is building a clockwork dragon. Eventually, we'll have hundreds of them. We'll use them to scout, conquer, and patrol this new frontier. But before that can happen, the test model must be completed. Sindri is almost finished, but to solve the last problem, he needs to study a real dragon. If you help us, we'll spare Ash and Stefan. You have my word."

I nod my head, curling up near the mirror to rest until the dizziness passes. In the back of my head, there's a nagging worry about something. I'm too dazed to figure it out. Gríma is a good person. Gríma is trustworthy. Gríma will watch over me while I rest.

After some time, I'm vaguely aware that night is falling. It was morning when I attacked the Svartr. How could so much time have passed already?

Below me, the ground shakes and begins to sink. It's pissing me off. I just want to lie here and be left alone until the dizziness passes.

In the back of my head, I feel like there's something I've forgotten, something I'm supposed to do. But I can't quite grab onto it.

## Apostles of Enlightenment

### Ash Kinley

As I stand outside of Eventide, the woman in a black robe approaches, carrying a book.

It's dark here, near the un-sun, but my wolf eyes can just make out her face. She's a Svartr, and she looks familiar.

I point my rifle at her and she stops about twenty feet away, calling out to me. "Hello, Ash."

It's Gríma! But she's not wearing her signature black face paint, and she looks almost … friendly.

I jump, adrenaline surging, as a figure darts in fast on my right side. It's Stefan! Like me, he's invoked and has his rifle pointed at Gríma.

Gríma turns calmly to him. "Hello, Stefan. Don't bother shooting. I'm already dead, and I have no wolf to threaten you."

He remains unconvinced. "We've heard about your mirrors."

Gríma shakes her head. "That's the Mirror Goddess, not me. I died over a thousand years ago, killed by a dragon. But my reflection lived on, and became one of the New Gods."

Still sighting my rifle at her head, I yell at her. "Why are you here?"

Gríma responds calmly. "Because I'm dead."

*She doesn't look dead.* "Why are you *here*, outside of Eventide?"

"Ah, now that is the right question. I like to read here. Can you believe I've learned how?" She holds up her book. "*Letters from a Stoic*, by Seneca. One of thousands of books in the Library of Existence."

"Did you know we were coming?"

"No. As I said, I like to read here."

Stefan's voice is flat and demanding. "Why are you in Eventide?"

Gríma smiles. "Another good question. Eventide is a place where certain dead, a fortunate few, come to learn the error of their ways, and live a life that nourishes the soul. But I'm guessing you two aren't dead, and you're here for other reasons. Anything I can help with?"

Stefan shakes his head, looking ready to pull the trigger.

I suddenly remember something Skadi said, that I might meet old enemies, now become friends. I whisper her words into Stefan's ear.

Stefan lowers his rifle but keeps it ready. "I don't trust you, Gríma. You're gonna have to prove yourself. Can you get us inside Eventide, and give us the layout?"

"Of course. We have an open society. You can come and go as you please."

I also lower my weapon. "Does Aud still rule here?"

Gríma nods. "Lord Aud may be old, but he's still a good ruler. He's read every book in the library. No one is more enlightened."

"Is he a god? What are his powers?"

"Lord Aud is a half-god, perhaps more human than god. He cannot read minds or see the future, but he commands the darkness and the magic of sleep."

*Why is Gríma being so helpful? Has she truly changed?*

"Gríma, tell us about Aud's artifact collection."

"He has many items in the Hall of Artifacts. Why do you ask?"

Stefan speaks up, lying. "A traveler mentioned the artifacts. We didn't really believe her."

Gríma's amber eyes sparkle with mystery. "All the legends are true, as you will soon discover. Come, I'll give you a tour of the castle. Perhaps you can meet Lord Aud."

Stefan and I share a glance. We're both thinking this is too good to be true.

*Are we walking into a trap? No, Skadi wouldn't steer me wrong. And why would anyone here want to trap us? No one knows we came to steal the Devourer.*

Stefan uninvokes and slings his rifle over his shoulder. I reluctantly do the same.

I'm having trouble trusting this woman. She doesn't seem at all like Gríma. But maybe death mellowed her.

Gríma hugs her book, looking pleased. "Follow me, then, and don't be afraid to ask questions. If you like it here, you may choose to remain and receive enlightenment."

*Okay, that creeps me out.*

As Stefan and I fall in behind Gríma, we exchange a quick hug and I whisper in his ear. "I'm so happy to see you. I had a rough trip here. You?"

He nods. "Not something I care to repeat."

Gríma sounds cheerful, speaking over her shoulder as she leads us to the enormous black gates of Eventide. "So, what brings you to Helheim?"

For a moment, neither of us answers, then I blurt out a lie. "I'm looking for my mother. She died of alcoholism."

Stefan gives me an inquiring look, but I wave him off with my eyes.

Gríma nods. "We get your type now and then. We call them *tourists.* I hope you find her, make your peace, and move forward. As Seneca says, every new beginning comes from some other beginning's end."

*Who is this Svartr? It can't be Gríma.*

As we approach the towering outer wall of Eventide, I notice it has a rough-hewn look, like it was hand-carved from obsidian. The iron gates, nearly as tall as the wall, rise a good forty feet from the ground. They're locked tight, but there's a small door open at the base of the gates and we walk right through.

If people can get in so easily, why bother with a big wall and iron gates?

The buildings inside are a mix of wood and brick, with the occasional stone cathedral. People from all races and all time periods walk the busy streets. Most appear blissful. None are in a hurry.

The weird thing is, despite all this activity, it's deathly silent here.

We begin walking up a long stone ramp that leads to the castle at the top of the hill. As we climb, our view improves, and I see a park down below, covered in purple grass and filled with exotic plants and trees I don't recognize. A few dozen people read in the park, none of them children. In fact, I haven't seen any kids in the city so far.

The beautiful castle, all black arches and sharp spires, rises above us as we approach. It's made of the same uneven obsidian as the outer wall. The building radiates a strange sense of peace, and I find myself yawning.

We pass through the castle's open gates. There isn't a guard in sight. Either Lord Aud doesn't care about his security, or he's very confident of it. The idea of trying to steal something from him is making me nervous.

Once inside, Gríma directs us down a long corridor to the right. She smiles, relishing her role as tour guide. "The first stop is always the Library of Existence."

This sparks my curiosity. "Weird name. Why's it called that?"

"The library houses every book written on the following three questions. How did I come to exist? What is the meaning of my existence? And what happens when I cease to exist?"

We turn left, passing under an open arch, and I smell the leathery odor of old books.

The library is a series of three towers, each open on the inside face, and each with a set of spiral stairs leading up through twenty or more levels of books. The stairs have an exit at each level that leads to a railed walkway around the wooden shelves.

Gríma looks proud. "I've read most of them, you know."

There must be thousands of books here. Tens of thousands. I doubt I could read them all in a lifetime. But of course, the people here have nothing but time.

At the center of the library is a series of reading tables, constructed of dark wood and lit by an occasional glowing sphere. Several dozen people pore over books. Some wear Greek togas, some Victorian dresses, and some jeans. But as I look closer, I see a number of people dressed in black robes, just like Gríma.

"Gríma, what's with the black robes?"

"The night robes are worn by the Apostles of Enlightenment, a path open to you, should you choose it."

*Is it some sort of cult?*

I glance over at Stefan, but his face is unreadable.

*I have to ask.* "What are the Apostles of Enlightenment?"

Gríma smiles. "That question would take hours to answer. But the short version is, we are people who have abandoned our vile impulses in order to pursue a deeper understanding of the world."

Gríma guides us out of the library. "I'm sorry we can't stay. You haven't been granted library privileges. That will come, should you choose to join us."

*Why does she keep mentioning that?*

We exit through the stone arch and back into the corridor. We retrace our steps, returning to the castle's gates, where we pass a group of dark-clad apostles on their way out. Some of them, clutching the sleeves of their companions, have completely black eyes, not a trace of white. From the looks of it, they're blind.

I whisper to Gríma after they pass. "What happened to their eyes?"

"Our most dedicated apostles ask Lord Aud for the gift of darkness. They believe that eyesight hinders inner reflection. Only when they are blind can they see. As for me, I've not yet summoned the courage."

*They blinded themselves? These people are nuts.*

When I look over at Stefan, he's nodding at Gríma as if he likes what he's hearing. Stefan would never drink the Kool-Aid. It has to be an act. I know he's had experience working undercover. I should try to follow his lead.

As tempted as I am to whisper to Stefan, to understand what he's thinking, I can't risk it. It's so quiet here that Gríma might hear us.

Another corridor brings us to a boring room filled with paintings and statues of famous scholars and leaders of the Apostles of Enlightenment. Gríma wants to talk about every one of them, and after a while, I can't take it anymore.

I interrupt her. "Gríma, will there be time to see the Hall of Artifacts?"

Gríma nods. "Oh, of course, right this way."

Stefan gives me the briefest look of disapproval, and I shrug in response. For some reason, I don't feel like hanging around in Eventide. There's something about the castle that's making me sleepy. Does Stefan feel it too?

Gríma leads us up a staircase of gray stone, and into a long, narrow room lit by glowing spheres held in sconces. Glass displays line each side of the hall.

My eyes fix on a display about halfway down the hall. I see glittering gems set in what looks like a human skull. The Devourer!

Gríma looks distracted as she leads us down the room's central walkway, covered with a crimson carpet threaded with gold. "I don't actually know what all these things are, but I'll do my best."

She skips the first pair of displays, one holding a silver helmet and the other a corroded sword, then stops at a glass case featuring a plain gold ring on a bed of black velvet. "That is Andvaranaut, the famous ring that makes gold. But of course, we have no need for gold here."

Despite her dismissive words, she casts a longing look at the ring before moving on.

Passing several more displays, she points to a giant ivory-and-gold horn that curves like a snake. "That is Gjallarhorn, trumpet of the Old Gods. Supposedly, you can drink from it, but I'm not sure how that's possible."

She passes several more cases without comment, including one with a gold-framed mirror. Stefan and I see our reflections in the mirror as we pass, but Gríma has no reflection.

I'm surprised when Gríma passes the Devourer with no comment.

Gríma and Stefan continue on as I stop for a closer look at the gem-encrusted skull. Why did Gríma skip it? Does she not know what it is?

Up ahead, I hear Stefan talking to Gríma, something about Achilles' armor, but I'm barely listening.

The skull is incredibly menacing, as if it's alive and about to crash through the glass to bite my face off. The idea of touching the thing makes me sick.

I must have been looking at it longer than I thought, because Gríma has finished her tour and is leading Stefan back to the exit.

I join them, trying to sound casual. "These treasures are amazing. So much history. They must be priceless. Why aren't they guarded?"

Gríma isn't put off by the question. "Guards aren't needed. The artifacts are protected by Lord Aud's magic, though it isn't necessary. We are his loyal followers. None of us would steal from him. And even if someone did, where would they flee? The dead are all prisoners of Helheim, and there's no place here to sell such things."

As Gríma leads us out of the hall, she's met by a feature-less creature made of shadow, hovering above the stone floor. It has something at the top of its body, vaguely head-shaped, that whispers to Gríma.

She turns to us. "I must end the tour. Lord Aud wants to see you now."

I feel my stomach flutter with nerves. I had hoped to avoid Lord Aud. I just want to snatch the Devourer and run.

Of course, Stefan is smiling, looking eager for his chance to meet the king of Eventide. Following his example, I force a smile.

Gríma points to the shadowy apparition. "Just follow the servant. It will lead you to the throne room. I'll catch up with you later."

Stefan shakes Gríma's hand and thanks her. I think he's laying it on a little thick, but I do the same. Gríma seems pleased by our reaction and leaves with a spring in her step.

*This whole thing is so surreal.*

The apparition begins to move, and we follow it.

The castle is big. We travel through a maze of corridors, most of them empty, but some traveled by dark-robed apostles.

I realize that Stefan and I, in our revealing slave rags, aren't dressed to meet a Lord. Also, no one has taken our faecast rifles with the sharp bayonets. They must be useless against the dead.

Suddenly, the apparition halts, and I see we're in the throne room.

It's a surprisingly small, dark space. Iron statues line the walls, each a startling depiction of a sleeping angel, all with unique faces. Their heads glow faintly, providing the room's only light.

A small man, hunched with age and cloaked in shadows, sits on an obsidian throne much too big for him. His head hangs, and he snores softly.

The apparition stands silently beside Aud, waiting for him to wake up.

Moments later, Aud's head lifts to face us. His raisin eyes twinkle in the weak light. He gestures us forward and we approach the throne.

I can't see his mouth, but his voice sounds broken and tired. "Welcome, travelers. What brings you to Eventide?"

*Gríma said he couldn't read minds. I hope that's true.* "I'm looking for my mother."

"Aren't we all? I find the first mother to be the most elusive."

I smile, pretending to understand him. "Do you know where I can find her?"

"No. Nor can I assist. You see, Helheim is a place within you. Eventide is the notable exception."

I nod. "Of course, Lord Aud. We're sorry to bother you. If we could just stay a bit, get our strength back, we'll continue on our way."

He cocks his head, vaguely amused. "I'm not sure that's wise. I know of a certain Dökkálfar who's looking for you."

My body tenses. *Does he know why we're here?* I force my voice to stay calm. "We've made a few enemies along the way."

"The dark elves are prickly, and so very different from all other Fae. Between you and me, I suspect they're not Fae at all. I've never seen such a relentless lot. Sindri won't rest until he finds you. And he *will* find you."

*I'm not sure how to respond.*

Thankfully, Stefan speaks up. "Lord Aud, Gríma says you're the wisest one here. Can you advise us on how to deal with Sindri?"

Aud nods his head to acknowledge the compliment. "There is one simple solution. If you opt to remain here, I can protect you from Sindri. And by remain here, I mean *forever*. The living aren't allowed to linger in Helheim. If you can leave, you must do so within a reasonable time. If you cannot, you must die and become a permanent resident."

*Die? You have to die to stay here? How exactly does that happen?*

Stefan nods, looking interested. "If we stayed, where would we live? In the city outside the castle?"

"Yes, or you could stay inside the castle and join the Apostles of Enlightenment."

*No freaking way.*

Stefan speaks, calm and smiling. "I'm impressed by what I've seen of them. I'm not saying I'm ready to join up, but I want to know more."

Aud looks skeptical. "Why, Stefan?"

Stefan takes a deep breath, as if remembering something painful. "On my way here, I met an old girlfriend, someone I screwed over a long time ago. Truth be told, I don't think about her much, but she thinks about me every day. I hurt her bad, then I got her killed. I can't risk doing that again, not to someone I care about."

He gives me a lingering, heartfelt look.

*And the Oscar goes to ...* Stefan Hildebrand. His act is amazingly good. So good that I find myself worrying. What if he's *not* acting? What if Aud cast a spell on him?

The thought of losing Stefan fills me with dread.

## GARDEN OF NIGHT

### STEFAN HILDEBRAND

THE MEETING with Aud went well, and now Gríma leads Ash and me down a long set of stairs that burrow beneath the castle.

Ash wears a worried look. Like me, she's agreed to explore membership in the apostles, but I can see this improvised plan of mine isn't setting well with her.

A soft bell chimes, seemingly from everywhere at once.

Gríma looks back over her shoulder. "That's the evening bell. The apostles will be gathering to eat and discuss their work. The next bell is the night call, when we sleep."

Ash frowns. "Why do the dead need to eat and sleep?"

"Some basic comforts are needed to pursue our work. They ease the mind."

Gríma leads us down a dark hallway, pausing at a wide doorway to a huge mess hall. Inside, several hundred dark-robed figures hunch over their food, whispering like they're afraid someone will overhear.

Gríma gestures to the tables. "I'd offer you something, but this food won't sustain living bodies."

As I scan the mess hall, I see no signs of servers, or any visible source of the food. As the apostles eat their beef and potatoes, the food replaces itself, so the plate always remains full.

Gríma continues down the hall, eventually reaching a series of rooms, each containing row after row of low beds with chests at the footboards.

"You will sleep in one of our community chambers. The beds with open chests are unclaimed. In the morning, you'll take your probationary vows, and a tutor will be assigned to instruct you in the tenets."

Ash's face hardens. "What vows, exactly?"

"Probationers are given three days to learn our ways and decide if this life is right for them. During that period, your only vows are chastity and obedience. If you elect to join us, there are other vows, as your tutor will explain."

*This gives me an idea.* "Gríma, we're willing to take the vow of chastity in the morning. But is it possible for Ash and me to have one last night together, somewhere in private?"

I take Ash's hand, avoiding her gaze as I look at Gríma with great sincerity.

Gríma seems taken aback. "Well, I suppose so. Provided you're serious about taking the vows, I could arrange an evening in the Garden of Night."

I smile. "Thank you, that sounds great."

Ash cocks her head at Gríma. "How do *you* do it? Remain chaste?"

Gríma stiffens. "It's not always ... easy. But as Seneca says, a gem cannot be polished without friction, nor a man perfected without trials."

Ash grins. "Seneca sounds like a sexist hard-ass. Come on, isn't there anyone from your past that you fantasize about? Someone who gave you some good ... friction?"

Gríma shakes her head, annoyed.

It seems out of character for Ash to be razzing Gríma like this. But maybe Ash knows what she's doing. Maybe she sees a vulnerability in Gríma that I don't. It'll be interesting to see how it plays out.

Gríma waves her hand, a gesture indicating the chastity conversation is over. She speaks over her shoulder as she heads back in the direction we came. "Come along, I'll show you the garden."

The trip to the garden is a short one, and we don't pass anyone along the way. After climbing a set of spiral stone steps, we reach the top of a spire, where we go out a door and emerge onto a suspended walkway hanging a good seventy feet above the ground.

The walkway sways unnervingly as we cross. It has no railing or rope handholds. I guess the dead aren't worried about dying in accidents.

We exit the walkway and step onto the enormous stone roof of a building near the castle. The space is square, each side nearly a hundred feet long.

On the opposite end, a spring flows from a fissure in a cliff rising above the building. From the drifting steam, I'd say it's a hot spring. Its water flows through the garden, collecting in an inviting pool, before the overflow runs through a stone channel and off the side of the building.

Ash gasps as she looks up. In the night sky, there are hundreds of stars, but I don't recognize any constellations. These are the first stars I've seen in Eventide. I'm guessing this is an artificial sky.

The garden itself has a few mossy clearings with small marble statutes of sleeping animals. I see a bear, a stag, and a raccoon. Between the clearings are rings of various flowers, all swaying in a phantom breeze. I don't know much about flowers, but these are unlike any I've ever seen. Their blossoms are rich and dark, covered with droplets of condensed steam.

Gríma seems unhappy as she waves an arm before her. "The Night Garden is yours. No one will interrupt you. But don't stay too long. Come find your beds when you hear the night bell."

Gríma marches back across the walkway and disappears into the dark spire.

I look into Ash's mischievous eyes. "What's with you poking at Gríma?"

"I'm unraveling a thousand years of her philosophical contemplation. Seneca, my ass. Gríma wasn't built to be an apostle."

I raise my hand. "Hold on, let's check this place out before we talk."

Ash nods. We invoke to heighten our senses, then walk around the garden, looking for anything suspicious.

There's no sign of danger, or anyone observing us, so we uninvoke.

Ash speaks as she hurries toward the hot springs. "Does Tyler have anything in his gear we can clean up with?"

"Hold on, I got us alone here so we could make a plan."

"Bath first, then plan."

I rummage through the pouch, coming up with some soap and a sponge, probably for cleaning the camp dishes.

When I look up, Ash is already naked and wading into the hot springs. She dips her slave clothes into the steaming water and wrings them out.

I once thought I saw Ash naked, but it was actually Mahna, pretending to be Ash. The body Mahna conjured was beautiful, but not as beautiful as what I'm seeing now. The real Ash has a few cuts and scrapes, and a couple of old scars. She's a fighter, a survivor, a tough girl who's somehow managed to keep a good heart. When I look at her, I see more than just an athletic body. I see an entire person, a person I want with every fiber of my being.

Steam coils around her, revealing flashes of her breasts. She looks at me with her irresistible half smile. "Come wash up."

My slave clothes aren't doing much to hide my erection, but Ash doesn't stare.

If I step into that hot spring, a lot more will happen than just washing up. Tactically, getting into that water is a stupid idea. We're in enemy territory. I devised a plan where we could be alone, and then sneak into the Hall of Artifacts to steal the Devourer. That plan is working, so why risk it by dropping our guard to have sex? It's irresponsible. I have a duty to perform here.

I think about what Elin said, that love is also a duty. But is this love, or just lust?

I already know I'm getting into that water, but the question is why? Am I being carried away by my emotions? Or is it something darker than that? What we're here for is incredibly dangerous: stealing an artifact from Aud and using it to kill Sindri. We could die. What if this is my last chance to be alone with Ash, to show her how I feel?

I put down my rifle and pouch, strip off my dirty rags, and head into the pool carrying my slave clothes, the sponge, and the bottle of liquid soap.

Ash splashes me playfully as I join her. "You look so serious."

"Not the first time I've been accused of that."

We wash our clothes with the soap, then set them on the moss to dry.

As we clean our own bodies, Ash asks for help washing her back. Before I realize it, the sponge in my hand is roaming beneath her tight breasts, and between her hard thighs.

She turns and we kiss, our bodies pressed against each other under the warm water. Her tongue darts here and there, soft and inquisitive, creating a powerful urge to invoke. But I somehow manage to control it. I can see in her eyes that she's fighting the same battle.

Somehow, it doesn't feel right to bring our wolves into it. This is just about me and her.

Ash's hand slips down between my legs, exploring my hardness, feeling my desire for her.

She whispers in my ear. "You know, those condoms are for more than gathering water."

I nod, surging out of the pool to tear open Tyler's pouch. I grab a condom pack and rip it open. My hands feel clumsy. I almost put the condom on inside out before finally getting it right.

I hear a splash as Ash emerges from the spring and joins me on the mossy bank. Her hard nipples press into my back, and her teeth nibble on my neck.

I turn around, sinking to the ground and pulling her on top of me. Without any awkwardness or a guiding hand, I slip inside her, like a lock and key, like we've done this a thousand times before.

As our bodies move in perfect rhythm, I feel a sense of awe and wonder, like the first time I invoked.

Ash whispers, "Oh, wow."

*She must be feeling it too.* "What is this?"

She whispers back, eyes wide. "I don't know."

Time passes in this sweet oblivion. I don't know how long. Then suddenly, Ash's skin flushes red, and her body quivers, tightening around me. My body releases a moment later, and we collapse into each other's arms.

For a long time, neither of us speak. As the spell fades, I reluctantly withdraw from her, becoming more aware of our vulnerability in the garden. It feels like waking up from an awesome dream. I just want to go back to sleep and pick up where I left off.

We share a silent kiss before rising to dress. Neither of us wants to say anything. No words can do justice to what we experienced.

Just after the night bell, Ash and I slip back into the castle. We pass no one on our way to the Hall of Artifacts. Everyone must be in bed. These people take their sleep seriously. I think it's something about Eventide itself. I've felt sleepy since I got here.

The plan is to grab the skull, wrap it in Tyler's space blanket, and stow it in the folded space pouch. Then we'll use the gate stones to escape the display room.

The only wildcard is Gríma. Will she come looking for us because we haven't shown up for the night bell? I'm not sure I buy her new personality. But maybe it makes sense. I'm a different person now than I was ten years ago, and Gríma has been here for over a thousand years.

As we approach the Hall of Artifacts, Ash and I invoke to enhance our senses. Neither of us spots any trouble. The castle is quiet as a crypt.

Concentrating on the mission is difficult. My body still vibrates from my experience with Ash, like a chime that rings long after it's struck. Her body acts like a magnet, pulling me in. She must feel it too, because her eyes are always on me.

We enter the Hall of Artifacts and stop in front of the glass display case holding the Devourer. Ash pulls out her gate stones and forms the circle that will take us back to Midgard.

We know that Aud has magic protecting these artifacts, but we're hoping our wolves can keep us safe long enough to get away. After we snatch the skull, it will only be a second or two before we leave. Of course, if Aud follows us to Midgard, then we have a problem.

Ash and I examine the glass case. Even with our wolf eyes, neither of us sees a way to open it. Maybe the best thing is to take the whole display box, though I don't know if the pouch will stretch wide enough to fit it through the opening.

In the hallway outside, a rustle catches our attention. We each crouch behind a display case. I leave my rifle over my shoulder. Best to use my claws if there's trouble. They're quieter.

Gríma, enters, her hands raised in peace. She whispers softly, but our wolf ears have no problem hearing her. "I'll help, if you'll take me with you."

Ash smiles smugly, as if she's been expecting this.

Gríma carefully approaches, speaking low and fast. "You have to hurry. The shadow servants patrol this area. They could be here any minute."

I stand and point to the case. "We need the skull. How do we get to it? We could break the glass, but I'm worried about the noise."

She shakes her head. "You can't break it or move it. But I can get inside."

Gríma hurries over to the display case that holds Andvaranaut, the ring that makes gold.

She pulls a black glove from the folds of her robe and puts it on her right hand. The surface of the glove shifts with many colors, like motor oil floating in a puddle of water.

She presses the glove against the display case, and the glass gives way, stretching like hot plastic as Gríma reaches in and grabs the gold ring.

Her body trembles as she pulls out the ring and kisses it. "I've waited so long for you."

Suddenly, Gríma cries out as her amber eyes turn to black coals.

She stumbles blindly toward us, her left hand holding the gold ring to her heart. "He's coming. We have to go!"

Ash's voice is hard. "Not until we get the skull."

Gríma sounds panicked. "But I can't see!"

I grab Gríma's black-gloved hand and place it on the Devourer's glass case.

"It's right here, Gríma, just reach inside."

Gríma pushes her hand through the glass and grabs the skull. The glass stretches like a rubber glove as Gríma pulls the skull out.

Somewhere, a bell rings three times, and I hear activity throughout the castle.

Gríma cries out, "We have to go, *now*."

I wrap the skull in the space blanket, being careful not to touch the damned thing.

I notice the black glove on Gríma's right hand is melting away, dripping onto the floor like black candle wax. But she doesn't react to it.

My heart pounds as my vision grows dark. *Am I being blinded?*

I look over at Ash, but I can't make out her face.

I shove the Devourer into the pouch and call out, "Let's move!"

Ash squeezes my hand and gives a warning: "Be careful not to kick the gate stones."

The truth is, I can't see them anymore. But I remember where they were.

Somewhere nearby, I hear someone shout, "Over here, my Lord!"

As tempted as I am to ditch Gríma, a deal's a deal. With my free hand, I lift her from the ground and hold her against me. I don't want her kicking the gate stones into disarray.

Together, the three of us move into the circle. At least I hope we did. I'm completely blind now.

# Metaphysical Trauma

## Tyler Buck

As I sink beneath the ground, an irritating sensation snaps me out of my reverie. An ant colony has broken open and the horrible little creatures are swarming all over my dragon feet. I have a sensitive ring of flesh above each claw that isn't covered with scales, and the little demons are biting me there.

I hate ants!

A memory suddenly hits me. I was talking to Gríma in a mirror! This hole beneath me is a dark elf trap. Why have I just been sitting here, letting myself get caught? Gríma must have done something to me.

When I try to climb from the deepening hole, my injured wing and broken leg radiate pain, weakening my entire body. I can't escape this trap.

Or can I?

There's still one option. I could try a time jump. But I'm weak, injured, and exhausted. Normally, a jump now would be out of the question. But if I don't try, I'll soon be part of Sindri's clockwork dragon experiment.

At least I'm in dragon form. That's my only chance of making this jump.

I shut my eyes, trying to block out the stinging ants and the pain in my broken body. I reach deep down, hoping I have one more jump left in me.

I concentrate on Professor Southam's anchor in the Academy garden. Without it, I'd have no chance of doing this.

A moment later, I feel the familiar falling sensation. The jump has started! Now all I have to do is make the landing.

It's a long jump back to the late Jurassic period. I had forgotten just how long. I start to slow down as I sense my approaching destination. I can see a garden. It looks like the Academy garden, but something's off.

Moments later, my dragon form emerges from the jump, hunched outside the mango grove on the south end of the campus.

I'm not inside the grove; there wasn't enough room for me in those trees. I'm just outside a huge iron fence. Each post in the fence is thirty feet tall and a foot in diameter. What happened to the unbreakable glass barrier that normally protects the garden?

I hear a noise behind me and turn my dragon head. Not far away, a spike-tailed stegosaurus, a little over half my size, retreats into the Jurassic forest. You know you're ugly when you scare away dinosaurs.

My body aches, and I'm on the verge of blacking out. If I revert to human form, it'll heal my physical injuries, and I may be able to squeeze between those iron bars and get inside the campus.

Without hesitating, I shift back.

I expected to feel a little better, but I don't. My body, if anything, has gone downhill.

I try to stand, but the ground jumps up to slam me in the face.

I *have* to get control of my body. Any moment now, an allosaurus could wander by and eat me for lunch.

Suddenly, I hear what sounds like squirrels giggling.

I look up and see a pair of familiar faces watching me through the fence. It's the two lower Fae, identical twins, that live under the Academy. They're sometimes called Brownies or Hobs. They are child-sized, with child minds, though they occasionally spout strange wisdom. It's unusual to see them active during the day. They're normally out at night, cleaning the Academy and stealing food. As Fae, they hate iron, so it's weird to see them so close to this fence.

Until they open their mouths, it's impossible to tell them apart. Both have brown skin, sharp teeth, wide noses, green eyes, and wild chestnut hair that seems to defy gravity. For modesty's sake, they wear loincloths, but I suspect they'd be happier without them.

One of them speaks, and I recognize him as 'Tisn't.

"Not one of we. Not not. Let the beasties eat him I say. Eat eat."

'Tis slaps his brother on the arm. "Yes one of we. Yes yes. Dragon man and time walker. Help him. Help help."

Their squeaky voices make me smile. I've missed them.

As I feared, they don't know me. In this damaged time-line, I was never born, and never attended the Academy.

Unable to get to my feet, I crawl toward the iron fence. 'Tisn't shrieks and runs away, disappearing into the mango trees. But 'Tis remains, mumbling to himself and wringing his hands. He wants to help, but can't risk touching the iron bars. Fae and iron don't mix.

If I'm gonna do this, it'll be without help. I climb to my knees, feeling like I'm going to vomit, and crawl to the fence. Up close, the thick iron posts are farther apart than they look, and I easily squeeze between them.

As I crawl onto the campus grounds, 'Tis hops around me. "Welcome, dragon man. Welcome welcome."

I forgot that Brownies smell like moldy cheese.

I bend over and dry-heave. That's always fun.

After the nausea passes, I sit against a mango trunk, looking out at the dirt corridor between two long rows of trees.

I spot Professor Damian Southam, with his leg braces and two walking canes, slowly making his way toward me. 'Tisn't, impatient with Southam's progress, circles around him, muttering something I can't hear.

I've learned to be patient with Southam. He's in his early forties and suffers from Hypermobile Ehlers-Danlos Syndrome, a disease that causes loose and unstable joints. Lots of students wonder why he hasn't traveled to the future and received the cure for EDS. I heard the reason is that his abilities are somehow linked to his disease. If he cures himself, he'll lose his powers. I don't know if that's true, but I do know one thing—the Academy can't afford to lose him.

Professor Southam, an Academy founder, teaches our most difficult courses, such as temporal twinning and dimensional ecosystems. He's also a time traveler. That's common here, of course. But Southam's ability to travel between alternate timelines makes him a dimensional traveler as well, the only one we have.

When he finally draws near, he's short of breath, and he says something I never expected: "Hello, Mr. Buck."

*This is freaking me out.* "How the hell do you know me? I don't exist in this timeline."

He smiles enigmatically. "How do you think I know you? Speculate."

"Hmm, either I'm back in my own timeline, which is impossible, or you traveled away from yours, which is very possible."

He nods. "I keep in touch with my alternate selves, though we're careful never to meet in person. We're aware of the breach. I'm just here temporarily, hoping you might visit. The resident Damian is holding my place back on my home timeline."

"How are things there? I don't suppose Rosemarie showed up."

Southam shakes his head. "Sorry, no."

I shake my head, trying to focus on the problem at hand. "What about Specta Aeternal?"

Southam speaks carefully. "What do you mean?"

"I know they've lost their presence on this timeline. Are they still okay at home?"

Southam's face tightens. "Why do you ask?"

"I was supposed to have a partner on this mission, but he went missing and was never replaced. SA told me it was a minor mission, that I could handle on my own. But it isn't. It's a fucking epic mission, and I need support."

The professor takes a deep breath, considering his words. "Specta Aeternal is a separate organization and I'm not privy to their communications. But I suppose it's obvious they're having … issues. Don't repeat this to anyone, but I've heard that many of their agents have gone missing."

I stumble to my feet, on the verge of collapsing. "What rumors? Which agents?"

"I'm sorry, Tyler, I don't have any details. Sit down, please. I can't help noticing that you're hurt. How badly?"

"Not bad. I just need a metaphysician for some quick work. My friends and I have a plan to repair the timeline. I'm supposed to meet up with them."

Southam's eyes fill with concern. "Oh dear. This version of the Academy is not as … evolved … as ours. They don't have a metaphysician. But fear not, I'll return home and fetch you one."

He waves at 'Tis and 'Tisn't, who are trying to climb a mango tree. "Get Tyler to the infirmary."

The Brownies scurry over and take positions on each side of me, supporting my arms. They're shockingly strong for their size.

When I look up, Professor Southam has vanished.

I must have passed out, because the next thing I know, I'm lying in a dark room. An old dark-skinned man with a long beard holds my hand. Candlelight dances on his face as he squeezes his eyes in concentration.

His eyelids suddenly flick open. "Hello, Tyler, I am Doctor Imamu."

I'm weak, but manage to nod.

He squeezes my hand. "You've endured a challenging injury."

"Is that a polite way of saying I'm fucked?"

He smiles, sadly. "I'm afraid so."

*I feel a sudden surge of adrenaline. Shit, am I going to die?*

"Look, I'll be fine, really." I try to sit up, but can't.

Imamu puts a comforting hand on my shoulder. But it's also a restraining hand. I'm not going anywhere.

"Tyler, listen to me. If flesh becomes gangrenous, it must be removed. Yes? The soul is no different."

"You're gonna cut away my soul?"

"Only that which cannot be saved."

"So what will that do? Bottom line me."

He crosses his hands, speaking softly, and I feel an odd sense of calm drift through me.

"Two of your abilities, time travel and dragon shifting, are at the level of grand disciplines, which means they've imprinted on your soul. When I remove the stricken parts of your soul, those abilities may be affected."

"Is there something like physical therapy, but for the soul?"

"There is. And that's a possibility. I'll know more once I begin the procedure."

I shake off the calm he's obviously projecting on me. "If I go through with this, what's the percentage chance of losing time travel? I need a number."

He smiles sadly. "I can't give you a number. All I can give you is my best work."

I eye him warily. "How good are you?"

He shrugs. "I was Professor Southam's first choice."

I try to whistle, but my mouth is dry, and it sounds like I'm trying to spit.

Imamu laughs softly, and I find myself wanting to laugh as well.

"Okay, Doc, give it your best."

He nods respectfully. "Are there any messages you'd like me to relay to friends or loved ones?"

*I understand the implication. I could die here!*

I take a deep breath and exhale. "Tell Southam he's my favorite prof. Tell Rose I love her. Tell Ash and Stefan I'm sorry."

He nods. "I will, if it comes to that."

Imamu reaches into a wooden tray and removes a thin metal disc. "Hold this under your tongue, please."

I do as he asks. The disc tingles, as if electrically charged.

He puts a similar disc under his own tongue.

Suddenly, for a moment, I'm looking down at myself through Imamu's eyes.

*Wow, I look like shit.*

My vision returns to normal as the doctor presses jeweled pins into various parts of my body. I don't even feel them.

Sleep engulfs me and I surrender to it.

I open my eyes.

I'm alive!

But where am I?

I'm staring at a spackled ceiling. Below it, brass wind chimes hang outside a window of thick old-fashioned glass.

I turn my head and see Professor Southam reading at a simple wooden desk. This must be his office at the Academy.

I try to speak, but all that comes out is a cough.

Southam jerks, startled, then turns to me with a smile. "Nice to have you back, Tyler."

"How long have I been out?"

"A day or so."

I sit up on a white couch of sorts, but it doesn't seem to have cushions. "How did the procedure go?"

He slowly turns his chair toward me, stopping for a moment to adjust the brace on his left leg.

He looks at me with eyes full of warmth and sympathy.

*Shit, this is gonna be bad news.*

"Tyler, you sustained significant metaphysical trauma. Doctor Imamu didn't think you would survive. I'm so pleased you did. That's a huge win."

I prompt him, "But?"

"But there was a complication. The part of your soul associated with time travel was damaged."

I feel like I've been punched in the gut.

"What do you mean, damaged? I can still get therapy for it, right?"

Southam looks pained. "Over time, we can explore that, but you need to manage your expectations."

I feel my adrenaline surging out of control. My skin begins to burn and I realize I'm shifting. But there isn't room in here for a transformation!

I stagger to my feet and throw open the window.

Southam calls out after me, "Tyler, wait!"

With his EDS, the professor can't get to his feet in time to stop me. I fall out of the open window, banging the chimes as I land in a garden of tall tropical flowers.

Fortunately, Southam's office is on the first floor, so the fall doesn't kill me.

As my fingers become claws, I realize there's barely enough space in this courtyard to contain my dragon.

A few moments later, I'm in dragon form, and ready to try a jump. I mentally picture the anchor I built in the present, at the place where I'm supposed to meet Ash and Stefan.

I feel a familiar falling sensation. I *can* jump.

But something's wrong.

Landscapes whiz past at a dizzying rate. I usually don't see anything during a jump until I'm slowing down at my destination. This jump is moving at light speed, and I have a bad feeling I've already passed the anchor.

I slow things down for a possible stop and see a nightmarish world of green metal spaceships shooting up from an underground city. They zip through a smoky sky and disappear.

This can't be right. I let this place pass, jolting forward for a while before slowing down again.

Now I see a swollen red sun swallowing a dry and blistered landscape.

What's happening to me? Am I hurtling toward the end of the world? It's like my time machine blew a tire and it's spinning out of control, heading toward a cliff.

# Mount Mansfield

## ASH KINLEY

My vision darkens as I step into the rune circle with Stefan and Gríma. Aud has blinded me, just like his apostles.

I'd hoped Seeker could protect me from Aud's magic, but even invoked, I've lost my sight. I feel sick and scared in a way I haven't since I was young.

What if Stefan's been blinded too? I pray he hasn't. It wouldn't be fair. I'm the one who got him into this mess.

I can't see where we are now, but I can smell smoke and fir needles. I think we're back in the real world, the world Sindri is destroying.

I pull Stefan into a desperate embrace and whisper in his ear. "Can you see?"

His answer tears my heart out. "No."

I choke down a sob as Stefan calls out, "Gríma, are you here?"

She doesn't answer. Guess she didn't make it through.

Suddenly, light strikes my eyes.

I gasp in relief as my vision returns.

I look into Stefan's smiling face. "Can you see now?"

He nods, hugging me tightly. Our rifle slings nearly slip off our shoulders.

I'm so grateful we have our sight back, but I can't help wondering why. Maybe Aud's influence doesn't extend to Midgard. Or maybe Skadi intervened. Either way, it's a wonderful feeling to see again.

Suddenly, something bumps into us. It's Gríma! She's come through the rune portal.

She clutches the gold ring in her left hand and reaches out blindly with her right, now without the black glove. "Did I make it through? I can't see."

She looks pale and stricken. I put a hand on her arm. "You made it. I think you'll be able to see soon."

"I had to fight to get here. Something wouldn't let me pass."

I lean down and quickly pick up the gate stones. I don't want anything following us here.

Gríma smiles at me. "I see you now! I can see my ring!"

She fondles the ring like a lover and touches it to her tongue. The contact makes her body shiver. "There's nothing like pure gold."

Stefan watches her, troubled, as she holds the ring up to the smoke-shrouded sun. "It will make *gold* for me. I'm not sure how. But it will."

Stefan and I remain invoked as we survey our surroundings. We're not in the same place as we left, but the rendezvous hill isn't far away.

The sun hasn't moved much while we were gone. It's possible that no time has passed.

Gríma yelps and picks up something from the ground. It's a human ear. She stares at in horror, realizing it's her own ear.

Then her nose falls off.

She cries out in anguish, "What's happening to me?"

We all know what's happening. Gríma is dead, and her body is falling apart. The magic that gave her the illusion of being alive was confined to Helheim. The dead don't belong in the world of the living.

Gríma reaches out to me, but her arm falls off. Then her legs crumble. She screams as her body collapses.

Stefan and I step away from the stinking cloud of decay as Gríma rots before us, eventually turning to dust. Even her black robe falls apart.

I shake my head, stunned by the sight.

Stefan leans down and picks up Gríma's gold ring. "You think Aud can track it?"

"I don't know. Maybe."

"What do we do with it?"

I think it over. "Gríma should have it."

Stefan nods and hands me the ring. He pulls the folding shovel out of the pouch, being careful not to touch the Devourer, wrapped in the space blanket.

Stefan digs a shallow hole where we place the ring with Gríma's remains. Then he covers the hole and stamps down the loose dirt.

I'm not sure how to feel about Gríma's death, or in this case, second death. I feel a little sorry for her, even though she tortured me at the Jotunborg. Did she redeem herself by helping us, or did she only do it to fuel her lust for gold?

As Stefan puts away the shovel, he tilts his head toward the nearby hill. "Let's go to the rendezvous point and make something to eat."

I realize now how hungry I am. "Sounds good."

I put my arm around his waist, and he wraps his arm around my shoulder. Together, we walk the short distance back to the hill.

There's no sign of Tyler when we arrive. I hope he's getting the medical help he needs.

We uninvoke and make camp high on the rocky plateau. Stefan fetches some water from the stream and we cook beef stroganoff on the propane stove.

I watch Stefan as he stirs our food, and feel fear growing inside me. I nearly got him blinded. I could have gotten him killed. I couldn't live with that. A world without him is my new vision of hell, even worse than the one with my drunken mother. I feel a powerful urge to protect Stefan, at all costs. Is there a way to get him out of this mess? Probably not. I can't kill Sindri without his help, and anyway, it's not my place to tell Stefan what to do.

I realize these are selfish thoughts. I'm worried about Stefan, yes, but I'm also worried about myself. I've already lost my dogs, and my parents, and Magnus. I couldn't bear to lose Stefan too. I think that would break me. Is this what love is? Does it make you fearful and self-centered? I can't let that happen. I've got to keep my shit together. I don't want to blow it with Stefan.

He looks at me, concerned. "You okay, Ash?"

I wave it off. "I'm fine. It's just … there's lots of stuff to think about."

He nods. "Yeah, me too."

*Does he know I'm thinking about him? Is he thinking the same things too?*

Stefan hands me a bowl of stroganoff, but I'm not hungry anymore. I feel so restless and wired up.

Stefan looks like he wants to say something, but he's taking his time about it. I know enough about men not to press him, and after another minute, he begins to speak.

"I've been thinking about our wolves, our vargr."

I nod, remaining silent.

"Seeker and Defender, they've been together forever, and they love each other, right?"

I nod again, my body tingling for some reason.

Stefan puts aside his food and stands, pacing around the propane stove. "Ash, maybe you already know this, but I think I should say something. The way Seeker and Defender are with each other, well, I'm starting to feel that way about you and me. And I'm thinking you might feel it too. I just need a reality check from you, to make sure I'm not crazy."

I smile, feeling giddy. "You're not crazy, Stefan."

I stand, ready to leap into his arms, but a shadow suddenly falls over the camp.

We both crouch, invoking as we grab our rifles.

The shadow passes and moves down the hill. It has a familiar shape. A dragon!

I look up as Tyler circles overhead, descending in a spiral and landing in the clearing below.

Stefan and I uninvoke. Stefan grabs Tyler's pouch and we both run down to the clearing. By the time we reach Tyler, he's standing nude in his human form, breathing heavily. One of his eyes is brown and the other lava orange.

I hug him, despite his nudity. I'm so happy to see him alive, even though he looks frazzled.

Stefan claps him on the shoulder and gives him the third set of slave clothes stored in the pouch.

Tyler talks as he dresses. "I missed the anchor, came out miles from here. Took me a while to find you."

I point to his dazzling orange eye. "What happened?"

"I somehow managed to lose a contact lens. Think I've got a spare set in my pouch."

Stefan hands over the pouch. "We added a sling so you can carry it on your shoulder. Be careful, the Devourer is wrapped in your space blanket. Try not to touch it."

Tyler nods, still looking a little dazed. He looks in the pouch, relieved when he finds his crystal claws.

I put a friendly hand on his shoulder. "Rough trip?"

He nods, "The worst. They managed to patch me up, but my jump awareness is fucked and I nearly got lost. When all this is over, I'll need some metaphysical therapy."

Stefan looks curious. "What's that?"

"Exercises for the soul, or some shit. I don't know. Do I smell lunch?"

Tyler slings his pouch over his shoulder as we lead him up to our campsite. My appetite has returned, and I enjoy some beef stroganoff while exchanging stories with Tyler.

His run-in with Mirror Gríma really worries me. If she's become some sort of mechanical monstrosity powerful enough to hypnotize a freaking dragon, what chance do Stefan and I have against her? We really have to stay away from mirrors!

After we eat, Tyler replaces his lost contact lens, and Stefan teaches him how to use our extra faecast rifle. Now that we're back in the land of the living, these strange guns can do some serious damage. Eventually, we'll have to stow them when we sneak into Dragonworks, but for now, it's best to have them at the ready.

We pack up camp and prepare for the hike to Dragonworks. Based on the information from the escaping slaves, Stefan thinks we can be at Dragonworks before dawn.

The plan is to use the mining aqueduct to get inside the underground city, then we'll make contact with the slave resistance movement. Hopefully they can help us kill Sindri, or more specifically, his soul. Although it's not part of the mission, I also wouldn't mind taking out Mirror Gríma.

After leaving camp, we travel southwest, heading for Dragonworks. Stefan takes the lead, with Tyler in the middle, and me at the back. I wanted to be next to Stefan, but he's good at this stuff, so I'm not going to question his reasoning. I'll do my best to make sure no one sneaks up behind us.

It's not a fun hike. The ever-present smoke is making my eyes tear up, and the slave sandals feel like torture devices. As we wind through the unending trees, I spot a mangy squirrel, who is obviously lost. None of the other animals want to be here. I don't see any deer or birds, and I don't sense any wolves in the area either.

About two hours into our journey, Stefan invokes and makes a silent signal for us to take cover.

I invoke, then Tyler and I crouch behind trees, rifles at the ready.

A figure emerges from the thick woods ahead. Shafts of dull sunlight strobe on him as he approaches.

It's Thayen! Sweat covers his brown skin as he half runs, half stumbles toward us. His deerskin tunic is ripped open, and blood trickles from claw marks along his chest.

He speaks in a low but urgent voice. "You're going the wrong way. Turn around."

He doesn't stop, and plunges into the forest behind us.

I realize I understood what the Mohawk said. Skadi's gift of tongues has finally kicked in!

Tyler watches him go. "Friend of yours?"

Stefan nods. "Thayen, the Mohawk warrior we told you about after you woke up."

"Didn't he have a whole band with him?"

Stefan nods unhappily. "Let's move on. Be on the lookout for an ambush."

Stefan and I stay invoked now. We're doubly careful thanks to Thayen's chilling warning.

About twenty minutes later, we approach a disturbing site. It's a clearing filled with colorful fall leaves, and lots of bodies.

Three Svartr females lie dead, broken spears jutting from their corpses. They're joined by the torn bodies of five Native Americans, probably Thayen's men.

Stefan nods respectfully at the bodies of the Mohawks. I know what he's thinking. How did this small group of human men manage to kill three invoked Svartr without using guns? The Mohawks must be awesome fighters.

Stefan speaks quietly. "Steer wide of the Svartr bodies. Don't look at their mirrors."

Tyler doesn't speak, but he looks angry and determined as we leave the massacre and continue toward Dragonworks.

After more painful walking, night falls, and we stop to rest. Stefan and I hadn't counted on needing to invoke so much today. We both feel the burn from using our wolves too long, and there's no way we can stay invoked for the whole night-hike to Dragonworks.

After talking it over, we decide to set up watches and sleep until midnight. We set up a fireless camp. Tyler says nothing when he sees me and Stefan sharing an air mattress.

Even if Tyler wasn't here, I'm too tired for sex with Stefan. But I do want to be near him. I know he feels the same way.

At midnight, we gather more water and cook a last meal before the push on to Dragonworks. This time, it's spaghetti, and it's the first camp meal I don't enjoy.

None of us talk. We're in enemy territory. The dark elves or Svartr could attack at any time, so we keep an eye on the gloomy woods around us. It's a warm and breezeless night. The smoke is stronger here, and I'm guessing it will get even worse as we approach Dragonworks.

When we finish our spaghetti, we pack up our things and move on, maintaining the same column formation.

We travel slower now. Stefan and I have invoked for better night vision, but Tyler can't see in the dark, so we have to guide him carefully around obstacles. Normally, I enjoy the forest at night. But not this forest. I keep expecting the ground to open up beneath us.

The hike takes forever. It's painful, tense, and at times, boring. But we finally reach Mount Mansfield about an hour before dawn.

Up close, the mountain has a faint yellow glow. Is that from the lava in the volcano, or is it light from the city beneath the mountain?

There's no obvious entrance. Fortunately, the slaves told us where to find the mining aqueduct, and if we hurry, we can get there before sunrise.

The trees around the mountain have been cleared. The area ahead is a graveyard of stumps. We'll have to travel in the open, and that makes me nervous.

Stefan leads us across the minefield of dry stumps, stopping every so often to crouch down and survey the path ahead.

As I kneel down beside one of the stumps, I notice that it's warm. There must be lava heating the roots. I wonder if that killed the trees. Maybe that's why they cut them down.

We continue our trek, passing through the field of stumps, and approach the bare ridge that marks the location of the aqueduct.

Stefan borrows the binoculars from Tyler's pouch and scans the mountain ahead. I hear him whisper, "Jesus."

*Something's wrong. Is it an ambush?*

Stefan passes the binoculars to me, and I see what alarmed him. Four people have been buried head-down in the ground, with only their feet and calves sticking up. Their feet are twitching. Those poor people are suffocating!

I want to sprint straight to them, but Stefan insists we circle around at a cautious jog.

Once he's satisfied this isn't an ambush, he signals for us to approach the victims. Their feet are still moving, so maybe we're not too late.

Tyler uses the shovel, while Stefan and I use our claws to free the first victim. It's an old man, the leader of the escaped slaves! Despite his jerky movements, he's clearly not alive. Clumps of black mushrooms quiver as they dig their roots into the man's mouth, eyes, and ears. The mushrooms have probably reached his brain, and that's what's causing the twitching.

Tyler whispers angrily, "This is some seriously fucked-up shit. Has dark elf written all over it."

Stefan shakes his head in disgust. "I think they're using these slaves as fertilizer to grow their mushrooms."

I jerk, startled as we hear a boom from the ridge above us. It's not like a gunshot; it's more of a wooden sound.

Have we been discovered?

# DRAGONWORKS

### STEFAN HILDEBRAND

I HEAR A DULL BOOM echo from the ridge. *What the hell was that?*

I immediately lead our group to cover in a ravine at the edge of the mountain.

Ash and Tyler look tense, but after thinking it over, I'm guessing the boom isn't directed at us. If we were going to be attacked, it'd be a quiet ambush.

My wolf nose doesn't detect any people in the area. All I smell is a chemical scent, kind of like a urinal cake.

The noise was probably from the mining aqueduct. Maybe it makes that boom when they turn the flow on and off. The smell may be some chemical they use in the mining, or perhaps an explosive.

The sun's coming up. We need to move fast, or we'll soon be visible from a mile away.

I signal for us to continue forward, trying to avoid Ash's eyes. She keeps drifting into my thoughts. I need to focus, or I'll get us all killed.

We climb around a stretch of boulders and stubby alpine trees, going slow enough for Tyler to keep up. As a dracoform, his human body is fast and athletic, but not fast enough to keep up with us wolves in the woods.

We crest the ridge just as the sun clears the horizon, bleeding red light into the smoky haze.

On the far side of the ridge we see the shallow aqueduct, cut from the bare rock. There's no water in it, only a thin layer of sludge that seems to be the source of the chemical smell. We're in luck, the water's turned off. But for how long?

My eyes follow the aqueduct to its source, a slot cut into the side of the mountain. The dark opening is so small that we'll have to crawl in on our hands and knees.

I speak quietly to the group. "We need to look like slaves now. Time to stow the rifles."

Tyler nods. "What about the pouches? Will they give us away?"

"I have no idea. Mine's not important. I'll stow it with the rifles. But you and Ash have to hold on to yours. You have the Devourer and Ash has the gate stones."

Ash has uninvoked. She speaks as she smears dirt on her face and body. "I have a question. When we kill Sindri's soul, he'll disappear from history and memory. It will be as if he never existed, and this timeline should return to normal. Sounds great, but what happens to Tyler's pouch and Skadi's gate stones?"

Tyler replies as he shoves the rifles into his folded space pouch. "There'll be a correction. We'll probably return to some previous point in this mission and we won't have any of the items we've acquired since then."

Ash sneaks a look at me. "Will we remember the things that happened here? Things we don't want to forget?"

Tyler pauses, understanding her meaning. "We might, since we're the travelers at the focal point of the changes. The more removed you are from the causation, the less you remember."

Ash nods, looking a little reassured.

I uninvoke and follow Ash's example, smearing dirt on my skin. Tyler does too, but I notice the dirt doesn't stick to his skin very well. Of the three of us, I look most like a slave, and Tyler looks the least like one. But Tyler might have the edge if we get caught.

"Tyler, have you had enough rest for a time jump if you need one?"

He concentrates for a moment. "Not a big one, no way. But maybe a small one."

I weigh the benefits of waiting a day before going into the mountain. It feels like the wrong move. Something tells me our time is running out.

It's time to go.

I'd love to deliver some sort of inspiring speech before entering the aqueduct, but we need to hurry. It's daylight now, and they could turn on the water at any time.

I head for the channel, gesturing for Ash and Tyler to follow.

We step into the aqueduct and our sandals sink through the sludge. My feet tingle and burn. They're using some nasty stuff in this mining operation. Hope it doesn't strip the skin off our feet.

As we crawl into the channel's dark opening, angled slightly uphill, the sludge gets on our hands and knees and makes my eyes water.

After crawling thirty yards in total darkness, another boom shakes our bones, and I feel cold liquid running over my hands and legs. They've turned on the water!

Ash and I could invoke and get out of here faster, but neither of us is going to leave Tyler behind.

We scramble up the slippery aqueduct as the incline becomes steeper. The water is up to my elbows now.

I hear Tyler call out from behind me. "You and Ash should invoke. Don't worry about me."

"Keep moving. It hasn't come to that yet."

Still, in my mind, I'm doing the math. If Tyler presses himself to the side, I think Ash could squeeze past him.

I feel a spasm of fear for Ash. What are we doing? She could drown in here! I should order our group to ride the water back out to the ridge.

But I never give that order. What's stopping me? Duty? Not that again.

The fear vanishes as I see dim light ahead. Moments later, we're able to stand.

We've entered a cavern lit by a few glowing glass spheres. Two male slaves, standing in profile to us, walk inside of a human hamster wheel that powers a gate mechanism. With each step they take, the aqueduct's gate lifts a little higher, and more water surges out.

The slaves stop as they see the three of us standing in the channel. Both men gape, as if we've emerged from the center of the earth.

The slaves wear clothes similar to ours, but they also have mirrors around their necks, an accessory we lack. Fortunately, the mirrors aren't facing us, and it seems the slaves are being careful to keep it that way.

Using my index finger, I give the secret signal of the resistance, scratching the skin over my heart.

The mining boss, a grizzled man missing half of his left hand, leads us toward a high platform overlooking the operation.

The vast cavern, easily two hundred yards across, is dimly lit by glowing glass globes powered by some unseen source. The mines are worked by dozens of men, women, and even children. All of them are wearing mirrors, and all are being careful not to face us directly. They're working together to shield us from the eyes of Mirror Gríma.

Across the cavern floor, dozens of shafts reach into the bowels of the earth. The miners navigate them by climbing ladders built into the shaft walls. When they emerge from a shaft, covered with sweat and grime, they drink greedily from buckets of standing water covered with a layer of dust. That can't be healthy. I notice that some of the miners are missing patches of hair, and others have open sores.

About half the time, miners emerge from a shaft carrying a pack full of dirt. They dump the dirt into the aqueduct, and the water carries the soil through a large metal filter before pouring out through the open gate.

It looks like a form of sluice mining, a process for collecting trace amounts of minerals, such as gold.

Watching the children work is pissing me off. One little girl emerges from a shaft with a fresh cut on her arm. She isn't crying. She just looks numb.

I glance back at Ash and see how sad and angry she is. She wants to run down and help the injured girl, but that isn't a good idea. One of the mirrors might pick us up.

As we stop on the observation platform, I notice that the mining boss isn't wearing a mirror. That's interesting.

Once we're on the platform, the boss gets in my face. "We can talk here. Tell me where you're from. Not from Dragonworks, that's for sure."

I was ready for this question, but I still don't have a believable answer. "We're from the Land of the Free. It's a long, long way from here."

He eyes me suspiciously. "Never heard of it. Show me the inside of your lower lip."

"What?"

"You heard me, pull your lip down."

I do as he asks, and he looks surprised when he examines the inside of my lip. "Okay, so maybe I believe you. But I still got questions."

*Time to press the offensive.* "We have questions too." I point to his neck. "Where's your mirror?"

"Took it off to talk to you. Mirror Gríma can't tell if I'm not wearing one. The only danger is a Svartr or sentinel seeing you without a mirror."

"Sentinel?"

The miner cocks his head impatiently. "The clockwork toads that monitor us. They're mostly in the city. They don't come out here much because the chemicals we use make them break."

"What are you mining here?"

He frowns. "The minerals they need for the clockwork projects."

"Who's guarding the miners?"

"There's usually a pair of Svartr at the water gate, but lately they've been missing shifts. Word is they're angry at the moles."

"Moles?"

His frown deepens. "The dark elves. Sindri's bunch."

"What's the issue?"

The boss shrugs. "Could be anything. This happens sometimes. That's how the last four managed to escape. Are they the ones who showed you the hand signal?"

I nod.

"They make it?"

I shake my head.

The miner scowls. "I warned 'em. It's more dangerous out there than in here. That's why change has to start *inside* Dragonworks."

"We want to help with that. We have a plan."

He pauses, then slowly nods. "What'd you have in mind?"

I suppress a smile of relief. It seems we've cleared the first hurdle.

The mining boss guides us through a series of tunnels that lead into a small room carved out of solid rock. On the other side of the room, the tunnel continues, but we stop here, and the boss unrolls a hand-drawn map of the city, flattening it over the closed lid of a heavy chest. He lifts one of the glowing orbs over the map so we can see better.

His dirty finger, black under the nail, points to a spot on the edge of the city. "If you continue down this tunnel, you'll come out here, near the goat pens, just at the end of the farm district."

"The tunnel isn't guarded?"

"We have tunnels the moles don't know about, for black market trade with the servant caste. Without that, we'd never get meat down here."

"What's our cover? Are we miners?"

He shakes his head. "The slaves here are divided into castes. I'm in the mining caste, so I'm not allowed in the city." He pulls down his lower lip to show a black dot on the inside. "Miners have black marks, court servants are green, city workers are blue, and house servants are red. If you get captured, they'll see you don't have a mark. Tell them you're one of the *unsold*, the orphans who grow up hiding in the tanning district. Unless they know who you really are, you won't be tortured for information. Nobody ever tries to sneak *into* Dragonworks."

"Why are the marks hidden?"

"Back before I was born, they used to be on the outside, but the castes took to fighting each other."

"What happens if they think we're unsold?"

"Then they sell you, of course. So don't get captured. Don't approach the sentinels, don't stop near the mirrors at the intersections, and avoid any slaves with faecast jewelry. Only court servants are allowed to wear sindrion, and those ass lickers are loyal to the masters."

Tyler speaks up. "What about the pouches we're carrying? Will they give us away?"

The boss shakes his head. "I've seen pouches before; doubt they'll be a problem. But you should clean up some before going in. You're not miners."

Ash raises her hand. "What about those mirrors everyone is wearing?"

He raps the heavy chest with his knuckles. "They're in here. Get them before you go. But when you're wearing them, avoid looking at each other face-to-face, and don't say anything that might give you away. She can see *and* hear through them. If you need to talk, go someplace where you won't be seen, and remove the mirrors. As I said, she can't tell if you're not wearing them. Look, it's not like she's constantly in these mirrors. There's tens of thousands of people in Dragonworks. In my whole life, she's only once spoken through my mirror, and it turned out she had the wrong person."

Ash steps into the light, pointing to her head. "Okay, one more thing. What about my red hair? I'm worried it stands out."

"Redheads aren't unheard of. We have a few. Shouldn't be a problem unless they know you're coming."

*Something's been lurking in the back of my mind, and I finally realize what it is.* "They may know we're coming."

All heads turn toward me as I continue. "Think about it. We traded clothes with those escaped slaves, then those slaves got caught. What will they make of that?"

The miner boss frowns. "Could be a problem. Make a head scarf to cover that red hair. There's rags in the chest. People will think you're a cook or a food server."

Ash nods. "Okay, sounds good."

The miner turns back to his map. "So you come out at the goat pens. Now head this way." His finger traces a line across the map, leading from the goat pens to a nearby area with many small buildings. "This part of Dragonworks is called the Servant Quarter. Most servants don't have their own homes, but some do. You'll need to find a woman named Thora. I don't know exactly where she lives, or what she looks like. But she's an important resistance leader, and she might know more about Sindri."

"Can I tell her you sent us?"

"She doesn't know me. And neither do you. There's a reason I didn't give you my name." He sets down the glowing orb, then rolls up the map and hands it to me. "You're on your own from here. The mirrors are in the chest, along with oil and linen to clean yourselves. Don't even think about returning through this tunnel. We'll be collapsing it after you leave."

I'm not carrying a pouch, so I hand Ash the map to stow in her pouch. Our hands touch, and I feel a little tingle of pleasure. Strange. That's never happened to me before. She smiles at me. I think she felt it too.

Tyler clears his throat, snapping us out of our reverie.

When I look up, the mining boss is gone.

Tyler opens the chest, putting a finger to his lips to remind us that Gríma can hear through the mirrors.

We use a pile of rags and a flask of moldy-smelling oil to get cleaned up. Ash also covers her hair. At the bottom of the chest are a half dozen mirrors on leather thongs, all lying facedown. We hang the mirrors around our necks, being careful not to face each other.

We continue down the tunnel in our column formation. This way, the mirrors only show our backs to Mirror Gríma, rather than our faces.

The tunnel grows darker and we have to find our way by touch.

The ground suddenly rumbles beneath our feet, and moments later, a cloud of dust sets us coughing.

The mining boss didn't waste any time sealing off the tunnel. Weird, though, I never heard an explosion. I wonder what they used to bring down the rock.

After a few more minutes of walking through the dark, we emerge into an open area. A black goat, chewing on a tuft of purple grass, glances up at us, then goes back to eating. Apparently, we're nothing to worry about. I hope everyone here feels the same way.

The light is dim, and I look around for the source. About forty feet above us is the city's ceiling. Hundreds of glowing orbs hang from the rock like huge stars in a suffocating sky.

It's too dark to see the city ahead, but I can make out most of this farm. The buildings are simple, all one-story, and seem to be made of a thick brown plastic material. The chimneys, however, are made from the green Fae metal. Thin white smoke rises from one of them.

I resist the urge to turn around and check on Ash. I don't want to expose her to my mirror. So instead, I gesture for us to keep moving forward. There's no need to look at the map again. The Servant Quarter isn't far from here.

I find a path skirting the farm, and we follow it past a few fungus gardens. The path is nothing more than bare rock. They probably had to haul in topsoil for this city, so any place without dirt can serve as a floor or a road.

We pass a few slaves doing farm chores, and I smell the stink of the animals.

After a few minutes of walking, we exit the farm district. The city is more congested. As we enter the Servant Quarter, the streets become wide, about thirty feet across.

There's no sign of motorized vehicles, but I do see a few coaches drawn by small, sturdy horses.

We pass a tavern, a butcher shop, and a bathhouse. The servant caste obviously lives better than the miners. Some of the shops have glass windows, and I glance at them on occasion, using reflections to check on Ash and Tyler. Both of them are keeping up and maintaining our column formation, and they manage to look casual while doing it. A worrying thought hits me. Can Mirror Gríma see us through these windows?

On each city block, a bored female Svartr stands guard with a faecast rifle. None of them look at us twice. As long as we're not causing trouble, we'll stay invisible to them.

There are no dark Fae in sight. Apparently, they don't mix with the rabble.

As promised, each intersection has mirrors on all corners, held up on posts, like street signs. I avoid looking directly into them.

I notice something odd that the mining boss didn't mention. In the center of each intersection, set into the rock, is a faecast plate about nine feet across. They look like giant manhole covers. I also notice that the slaves never step on them, and the coaches avoid them. What's up with that? Following their example, I make sure our group gives them a wide berth.

The most troubling feature of Dragonworks is the sentinels. The huge, unmoving clockwork toads, with mouths bigger than a man, sit atop brick towers, about twenty feet high, scattered randomly around the city. The faecast toads have unblinking, mirrored eyes, and it's impossible to tell if they're looking at us. If the miner boss hadn't warned us about them, I might think they were giant gargoyles made to scare kids on Halloween.

A female slave, wearing a clean robe and a faecast circlet, hurries through the street. People part to make room for her. Like everyone else, she ignores us. I'm guessing she's one of the court caste.

The shops are starting to thin, giving way to residences. This is the area the miner boss wanted us to visit, the place we'll find Thora. It's probably time to start asking around about her.

Suddenly, I hear a whoosh behind me, and Ash cries out. I flip my mirror, so the reflective side is against my chest, and turn toward her.

That's when I see that Tyler has vanished.

Ash stands in shock, her hand over her mirror, pointing to a nearby intersection. A giant manhole cover has moved aside, and one of the sentinel toads is squeezing down a metal tube that runs beneath the street.

Ash speaks in quiet horror. "It's got Tyler, in its mouth."

I feel frustrated and helpless. I have no weapons to fight the sentinel. I could invoke, but that would grab the attention of the armed Svartr, not to mention the other sentinels.

I scan the area around us, looking for a shop we can duck into. That's when I see another sentinel leap from its perch. I hear a whoosh as its tongue flashes out at a blinding speed, wrapping me up and yanking me toward its maw.

The impact knocks me out for a few seconds. When I come to, I'm in the creature's mouth. I peer out through its slitted lips and see the toad descend into a pipe leading below the street.

I can't move. The sentinel's powerful tongue, built like a bicycle chain, keeps my arms pinned to my sides. I invoke and try to break free, but this beast is incredibly powerful, and I can't wiggle loose.

Fuck.

I hope Ash escaped. If she gets hurt, I'll find a way to tear this place apart and shove the pieces up Sindri's ass.

## Onion Cellar

### TYLER BUCK

I THINK A SENTINEL grabbed me. I caught a glimpse of it as it sucked me into its mouth. Man, what a wild ride. My whole body aches.

I can't believe I'm still alive. The clockwork toad is probably designed to capture rather than kill. At least I've got that going for me.

I'm worried that my timesight didn't kick in as I was being reeled into the toad. It wouldn't have helped anyway, as I was caught by surprise, but it was disconcerting that I wasn't able to see multiple images of the toad. In training, Gammachu said the ability works against animals and people, but he didn't say anything about clockwork creatures.

I peer out from inside the slit of the creature's mouth. I'm guessing it keeps its mouth cracked so I can breathe. Looks like the toad is crawling under one of the giant manhole covers. Is it taking me into a sewer?

My arms are pinned by the sentinel's metal tongue, hinged like chainsaw chain. It's getting hard to breathe. The more I fight, the harder it squeezes. My ribs feel like they're about to crack, and I'm getting tunnel vision.

How do I get out of this? There isn't room in here to shift into dragon form. I still have one option, but it makes me nervous. I can time shift. I really haven't had enough rest since my last ridiculous jump, but a tiny jump now, just ten minutes into the future, might be possible. Hell, I was making those kinds of jumps in training, before I knew what I was doing. Still, part of me is afraid I'll land a billion years in the future, long after the sun has swallowed the earth. I don't think any temporadi has ever jumped into the sun. Maybe I'll be the first.

I feel a falling sensation as the jump kicks in. A split second later, I'm lying in a dark, circular tunnel with smooth metal walls.

I think it worked!

I walk up the tunnel's incline until I find the giant manhole cover. I'm sealed in from the street above. Even if I could lift this massive lid, there's nothing on the other side but more sentinels, not to mention Svartr with rifles.

I've got to get moving. If one of those toads tries to squeeze through here again, I'll be crushed, or swallowed.

I've still got my pouch, and inside it, the faecast rifles and my crystal claws. But I'm not certain either will stop the clockwork toads.

I descend into the metal tunnel, feeling my way through the dark, searching for a safe way back to the surface.

I hope Stefan and Ash are okay. I wonder why the sentinel attacked. There must be something about my costume that's unconvincing. Or maybe it could sense I wasn't fully human.

About thirty yards down, I find an open hole in the side of the tunnel, about ten feet across. I step through it and see light up ahead.

After passing through a wide corridor, I emerge in a huge workshop lit by glowing spheres.

Several dismantled sentinels squat at workstations, their mirror eyes closed as human slaves clean their parts and oil their mechanisms.

I'm guessing these people must be from the city worker caste. They wear leather pads protecting their knees.

I see no guards here, and no one is paying attention to me, so I steal a pair of kneepads from a nearby table and slip them on. Then I grab a basket of tools and walk across the shop, trying to look like I know where I'm going.

When I reach the far side of the workshop, I realize I was wrong about the lack of guards. A female Svartr with a faecast rifle leans against the wall in the shadows, looking half-asleep.

My pulse quickens as I approach her.

I pass her and she barely looks at me.

I find the exit and walk out into a long hallway cut from the raw stone. Ahead, on my right, there's an open arch with warm light drifting out.

I'm hoping it's a stairway leading to the surface, but no such luck. I look inside and see a small chapel, lit by many tiny globes.

There's no service going on, but several well-dressed slaves sit in the pews, their heads bowed to an idol up front. It's a gold statue, about two feet tall. I'm seeing it at an angle, so it's hard to tell, but it looks like a dark elf. A *clockwork* dark elf.

Something tells me these people are praying to Sindri.

One of the worshippers stands to leave. I see a faecast ring on his hand. Must be in the court caste.

He snaps at me as he passes. "Pray or depart. But don't gawk."

I nod, feigning fear and embarrassment. The man leaves, looking satisfied at putting me in my place. Prick.

As I look at the clockwork Sindri statue, I remember when I saw Gríma in the mirror, and how she looked metallic. Have Sindri and Gríma both moved into clockwork bodies? That could explain why they're still alive over a thousand years later.

I think Ash told me that the Devourer had to touch Sindri's blood. Does the dark elf even have blood now?

I've got to get this information back to Ash and Stefan. I hope they've managed to find Thora.

I continue down the corridor and follow a bend to the left. I tense as I hear crying ahead.

Moving cautiously forward, I peer into the gloom and see a trio of slaves being herded by a pair of Svartr with rifles.

One of the slaves is an old woman, the second a man in his thirties with a badly injured leg dragging behind him. The third slave is a teen girl with a horrible rash on her face. None of them are wearing mirrors.

The Svartr unlock an iron door and lead the frightened slaves down a set of stairs. The teen girl cries and the man calls out, "Spare us, I beg you!"

Are they being executed? Why? Maybe Dragonworks only wants young, healthy slaves.

My body jerks at the sound of a gunshot, followed by the growl of angry Svartr.

Have the slaves been killed? No, I can still hear the girl crying. I'm guessing the man fought back and they killed him.

I've got to help them. It could cause problems for me, but it's the right thing to do. Besides, maybe the slaves can help me get to Thora.

I put down the tool basket and reach into my pouch. I draw out a faecast assault rifle, walk over to the open iron door, and head down the stairs.

I pass the body of the man with the bad leg, what's left of him anyway. It looks like the Svartr ripped up everything *except* his bad leg.

As I descend the narrow stairway, the air becomes thicker.

Eventually, the stone stairs lead to a small cavern lit by glowing green moss. I gag at the stench of blood and death, but I can't see its source.

The two Svartr emerge from a tunnel on the other side of the cavern. Their faces are drenched in blood. They're headed straight for me but haven't noticed me yet.

I lift the rifle and fire twice into the biggest one, now only twenty feet away. She drops, but the other one invokes, raises her gun and fires.

My timesight has kicked in, and I'm already in motion, shooting again as I dive to the ground. The first bullet hits her head, dazing her and killing her wolf. That was a lucky shot. The second two bullets miss.

She recovers and fires again, but I've already rolled behind the cover of a rock formation.

She screams in fury and I hear her charging me. Her rifle has a bayonet and she plans to use it.

I drop my rifle and pull my crystal claws from my pouch, barely getting them on before she steams around the formation, driving the bayonet at me.

Without her wolf, she doesn't have a chance. I see where her bayonet is about to strike. I bat it aside with one hand and slash her throat with the other. She dies at my feet, gasping for air, eyes wide with shock.

Will the gunfire attract more Svartr? Maybe not. After all, they did shoot the slave on the stairs, and nobody came running.

I sling the blood off my claws and stow them away. Then I pick up my rifle and cross the small cavern. The stench of death grows stronger as I pass the other dead Svartr and walk through an opening into a huge cavern.

Here, I see the most disgusting sight of my life.

Huge maggots, with toothy, suckered mouths at least six inches wide, writhe inside the wall's honeycomb chambers. Withered and pale human slaves hang before the chambers, bound by faecast chains. The maggots' maws reach out to suck blood from these sacrificial slaves.

I feel like puking.

Most of the victims have been dead for a while. The old woman, a maggot sucking at her back, looks to be unconscious.

The teen girl, paralyzed with terror, makes a soft keening noise while a maggot tears away the tunic over her kidney.

I lift the rifle and fire at the maggot attacking the girl. It makes a whistling noise through its mouth as black blood spurts from the wound, then it shrinks back into the gloom of its chamber. Hopefully, it's dying in there.

I also fire a bullet into the maggot draining the old woman, then I rush over and check her for a pulse. She's dead. I doubt the maggot killed her so fast. It was probably a stroke or heart attack.

As much as I'd like to shoot every maggot in this godforsaken cave, I need to conserve my ammo.

The teen girl is the only one left alive. I don't have a way to unlock her manacles. I could shoot the chain connecting them to the wall, but that would risk a ricochet. So instead, I take out my crystal claws and try to slash the chains apart. My first attempt fails, but I think it's because I wasn't pulling the chain rigid enough. I try again, and manage to cut through. The girl collapses into my arms, sobbing.

I whisper to her, "What is this place?"

She speaks between sobs. "A dark elf ... nursery. There are hundreds of these places."

"Wait, you're saying the maggots are their children?"

She nods. "After a few weeks, the maggots harden, and the baby elves break out of the shells. Until then, they need blood. Lots of it."

I hold her at arm's length so she can get a good look at me, then I use my index finger to scratch the skin over my heart.

She gives me a wary look. "Thanks for saving me, but I'm not part of that. They're going to get us all killed."

"I'm here to make sure that doesn't happen. Can you tell me where to find Thora, or any of their other leaders?"

"I don't know any Thoras. But I hear Valda's one of them. She's Svartr."

"The Svartr are part of the resistance?"

"Not most of them. But a few."

I watch her eyes to see if she's lying, but she seems sincere.

"I'm Tyler. What's your name?"

"Splotch."

"Your real name."

She looks embarrassed, tilting her head to hide the rash on her face. "That *is* my real name."

This poor girl never had a chance here. Sindri has a lot to answer for. I'm going to enjoy taking him out.

The girl suddenly screams and points behind me.

I spin around with my finger on the trigger, and see what must be a female dark elf, nude and covered with mud. Her pointed ears twitch with alarm as I fire. But I know the bullet won't hit her. My timesight shows her disappearing into thin air, and so she does.

From my training at the Academy, I know that High Fae can travel into Som, a reflective plane where time passes slower. If that's where this one went, time is on my side now, and I'll be gone long before she can reach help.

I turn back to the girl. "Take me to Valda."

The girl frowns, then gestures for me to follow her. We leave the way I came in, climbing the stairs and emerging into the empty corridor.

I suddenly realize that I'm wearing my mirror! The Svartr I killed were also wearing mirrors. Shit. Mirror Gríma might have seen all of this.

I guess that's water under the bridge now. I'll keep wearing my mirror. Don't want to attract unwanted notice from passersby.

I put my rifle in the pouch and speak to the girl. "Should you be wearing a mirror?"

"No, they take them away when they're about to kill us. Just hold the chain hanging from my hand. Pretend you're leading me somewhere."

I nod, following her instructions as we begin walking down the corridor. The ruse works. We pass a couple city workers, and someone from the court caste. No one gives us a second glance.

We emerge into an immense open space, a whole new level of the city. We're standing at the top of a stone ramp that runs down the side of the wall that encompasses the entire level.

As we descend into the city, I see a lot of small buildings, closely packed. Amber-eyed Svartr move through the streets. Unlike what I've seen previously, some of them are male and some are children.

I'm guessing these are the suburbs where the Svartr live. Weird. They never seemed like the indoorsy type. Then again, a lot of time has passed, and things change.

We exit the ramp and enter the Svartr community. Here, there are no guards or sentinels. I spot a few human slaves, but they're definitely in the minority.

The girl, I hate calling her Splotch, directs us to a little house made of the same brown plastic that I saw on the upper level. It's an out-of-the-way structure along the edge of the level.

As we approach the house, I remove my mirror and drop it facedown in a nearby mushroom patch.

The girl points to a stuffed rabbit head over the door of the house. "This is Valda. The bunny place."

"Do you know her? Will she answer if you knock?"

"I don't know if she'll answer. I only met her once. My older brother used to serve her. He's the one who told me she hates Sindri."

We approach the door and the girl knocks softly with a trembling hand.

Almost instantly, the door flies open, revealing a graying Svartr woman in a belted beige robe. I notice she isn't wearing a mirror.

She eyes us suspiciously, then softens as she studies the girl. "Splotch, is it?"

The girl nods.

I use my index finger to scratch the skin over my heart, but Valda shows no sign of recognizing the gesture. She makes a shooing motion with her hand. "This isn't a good time. I'm busy making soup."

The girl, abashed, turns away, but I stand my ground. "Valda, could we please come in before another sentinel swallows me whole?"

Valda's eyes fill with curiosity. She takes a step back and motions us inside.

The girl doesn't want to enter. I have to give her a little push.

The air is warmer inside, and I smell mushrooms cooking.

The one-room house is tiny, lit by glowing glass spheres. I see a pot boiling on a coal-fired stove. Beside it stands a cabinet covered with jars of spices. In the corner, there's a low bed with some yellow rabbits painted on the wall around it. *What's with the rabbits?*

Without explanation, Valda picks up a wooden staff in the corner and raps it against the floor three times.

I look warily into her amber eyes. "What's that about?"

She looks amused. "Chasing away evil spirits."

She puts down the staff and stirs the pot with a wooden spoon. "You like onions?"

*What's her game?* I shake my head. "Thank you, but we're not here to eat."

The girl eyes the door. I'm still holding the chain around her wrist, afraid she'll bolt.

Valda speaks, as if reading my mind. "You can release Splotch. The door only opens to my touch."

*That's interesting.* "You're saying we're your prisoners?"

"I'm saying I need onions. They're down in my onion cellar. Be a good boy and fetch me some."

She points to a rug on the floor. I move it aside with my toe, revealing a trapdoor.

*For some reason, this woman has a witchy quality, and there's no fucking way I'm going down there for onions.*

Without realizing it, I release the girl. She's already at the door, but it won't open for her.

I pull a rifle from my pouch but keep it pointed at the floor.

Valda, unfazed, continues to stir. "I don't allow weapons in the cellar. You'll have to leave your things with me."

I laugh coldly. "There are no onions down there."

"There could be. You'll never know if you don't check."

The girl sits against the door, crying.

Valda frowns at me. "You've upset Splotch."

Anger flares in me. "You're the one with the door that won't open!"

Valda takes a spoonful of soup and tastes it. Her nose curls. "I'm getting sick of mushrooms. I must insist you fetch me an onion."

I suddenly realize why she rapped the staff on the floor when we first came in. "There's somebody down there. You alerted them."

She sighs, exasperated. "You're new here, so I'll explain something. The resistance began two years ago, when the Dökkálfar executed a starving slave who stole an onion. Onions are rare down here, you see. I can't afford them."

"Ah, so when you're talking about onions. You're not really talking about onions."

"Now you're getting it. Your rifle and pouch, please."

She steps over to me and holds out her hands.

*Is she really with the resistance, or is this a mind game, a clever trap?*

I look over at the girl, but she's no help. She's staring at the door, chomping on her thumbnail like a beaver.

I don't know what to make of Valda. It seems unlikely that a Svartr would be in the resistance. On the other hand, she's my only lead, my only possible way of reconnecting with Ash and Stefan. So she's probably a risk worth taking.

Slowly, reluctantly, I hand my rifle and pouch over to Valda.

She nods toward the trapdoor. "Go on down. They're waiting for you."

"Who's waiting for me, exactly?"

"People who can help."

She sets my stuff down in the corner and goes back to stirring her pot. She really looks like a witch now.

Annoyed with her games, I march over and throw the trapdoor open. I see rickety wooden steps leading down into darkness.

I pause, having second thoughts.

*Stop hesitating. Just do it. Stefan and Ash would do it for me.*

I slowly descend the creaking stairs. They go on longer than I imagined. When I reach the bottom, the trapdoor slams shut above, extinguishing the last of the light.

If I go back up, will the door be locked? I'm really cornered down here. I haven't rested long enough to make another time jump.

Suddenly a glass sphere begins to glow near my feet. At the edge of its light I see three figures, clad in black, with faecast rifles pointed at me.

Dark elves!

Fuck, I really walked into this one.

# AUCTION

## STEFAN HILDEBRAND

I'M LEARNING how the toad thinks. It's afraid of killing me. If I stay perfectly still in its mouth and breathe shallowly, the sentinel's tongue loosens around my body and the pain subsides.

I can't escape this creature, even with Defender's help, so I decide to uninvoke. I'm being transported somewhere, and when I arrive, I don't want to be in wolf form. It's possible they don't know who I really am. I need to stick to the story of being an unsold slave from the tanning district.

The sentinel pushes its way down a series of underground pipes, occasionally turning or descending. Eventually, we stop, and I hear the faint whir of gears as the toad's mouth opens.

The creature spits me out. I spin as its tongue unrolls, dropping me hard on a stone floor and knocking the wind out of me.

I'm in a domed chamber cut from stone. Four female Svartr, all young and strong, all with black body armor and faecast rifles, stare down at me with curiosity. One of them has a white scar across her lips. She grabs a fistful of my rags and drags me to my feet. "What happened? Why did the sentinel take you?"

*That's a damned good question. Could it tell I'm Were?*

I have to give these Svartr a lie they'll believe. Time to test out my cover story.

I pull down my lower lip, showing that I don't have a mark.

The scarred Svartr raises her eyebrows. "Unsold. We haven't had one of those in a while. You're from the tanning district?"

I nod.

"Then I'm sure you can tell me the name of the tanner who makes those expensive fox pelts."

*She's testing me. Shit. I wish the miner boss had told me more about the tanning district.*

I open my mouth awkwardly, stuttering and drooling, and blurt out something incomprehensible.

The Svartr frowns in disgust. "They should cut out your tongue if you can't use it right."

As tempted as I am to invoke and attack, that would be foolish. These are not normal human women. They are Were, with powerful wolves, effective armor, and devastating firepower. Having already fought them, I know that any heroics right now would get me killed. I have to keep pretending I'm a slave and wait patiently for a chance to escape and find Ash.

The scarred Svartr grabs me by the neck, flanked by her three fellow Svartr as she pulls me to the open door of the domed room.

I took a guess that some of the orphans who grow up in the slums here, probably without health care and schooling, might suffer from disabilities. I must have guessed right, because the Svartr seem to be buying my act.

They take me across a street crowded with a mix of Svartr and slaves. Most of the Svartr are unarmed and wearing civilian clothes, such as robes. To my surprise, a few of them are men and children.

I only see two sentinels squatting on their brick towers. They're less frequent here, maybe because there are fewer slaves in the streets.

After crossing the street, we pass through a faecast gate into a fortified area, surrounded by a ten-foot-high stone wall. Most of the Svartr inside don't have armor, but they do carry weapons I haven't seen before: short shotguns with three-inch-wide barrels. Not shotguns, more like hand cannons. I'm guessing they fire giant beanbag rounds that disable the slaves without killing them.

We pass a series of stockades holding human slaves. One of them is filled with old people. A man sits in the corner with his head in his hands, pleading to no one in particular, "Not the nursery. Not the nursery!"

Up ahead, a pair of Svartr pull a teen boy away from his slave parents. His mother falls to her knees, begging. "Please, he still has one year left!"

Suddenly, the panicked boy makes a break for it, running past me.

One of the guards lifts her hand cannon and fires. A tar-like ball hits the boy in the back with a wet smack. The ball flattens like a pancake, delivering enough force to knock the boy down, where he's quickly swarmed by Svartr.

I look around for Ash and Tyler, wondering if they've also been captured and taken here. But I don't see them. I hope that's a good sign.

My four guards lead me to a raised platform, where they draw a pair of manacles from a metal box. It takes some willpower to let them shackle me, but it's necessary. The faecast chain doesn't look very thick, but I'll bet it's strong. Even invoked, I'm not sure I could break it.

Three of my Svartr escort leave, including the scarred one. The remaining Svartr, a young woman of maybe twenty, leads me up the stairs and onto a platform. A closed curtain runs across the center of the platform, so I can't see what's on the other side. But I can hear what sounds like an auction.

I now realize I've entered through the back of a slave market. This is actually good news. They're going to sell me rather than kill me.

An overweight female Svartr, one of the first heavy ones I've seen, pushes through the curtain and hurries toward me, her gray robe flapping behind her.

She checks my lower lip, then squeezes my limbs. She peers into my face, curious. "I don't understand you. Most unsold are sickly and thin. You're built like a warrior. Where are you from?"

Once again, I mutter something incomprehensible.

She frowns. "I don't suppose you can write?"

I shake my head.

She pulls a small leather-bound journal from her robe and checks a few pages. "Hmm, I think the city benefits most from selling you to private buyers. You're strong and quiet, so maybe a farmhand."

She produces a faecast pen engraved with a spiderweb pattern and makes a notation in her journal. Then she disappears back through the curtain.

I wait with my Svartr guard for about ten minutes before anyone else approaches. This time, it's a pale male slave with a small knife.

My jaw clenches as he extends the knife toward my gut. I resist the urge to defend myself. After all, why would he be trying to kill me?

The slave slits open my filthy tunic and tears it down to my waist, exposing my upper torso. That makes sense. The buyers want to see the merchandise.

The slave speaks, his face nervous. "We're passing you off as mute, so don't babble while you're out there."

I nod and he darts back through the curtain.

A few moments later, the gray-robed Svartr emerges and takes custody of me, leading me through the curtain and out onto a wooden stage, well lit by a ring of large glowing spheres. On either side of the stage stands an armored Svartr with one of the wide-barreled guns.

Looking out beyond the stage, I see a small, dark amphitheater. The seats are mostly empty, with only a half dozen female Svartr present, all in civilian clothes. These must be the private buyers.

Suddenly, something approaches from a ramp running down the center of the amphitheater. It's a small litter carried by a pair of burly slaves. I can't see who rides in the litter; it's covered with a canopy of black velvet.

The slaves set the litter down at the base of the stage.

Immediately, five of the six buyers stand up and leave. Only one buyer remains. She's a middle-aged Svartr with a shaved head and a single dangling faecast earring. She had been sitting in the middle but now moves to the front row. I notice that she wears a prosthesis, a clockwork left hand. Did she lose the hand in a fight? Why did she remain here when the others left?

I'll bet the person in that litter is a VIP. But the bald Svartr is probably equally important. I'm not sure who I want to win this auction.

The gray-robed Svartr bows to the buyers. "Thank you for your interest in this recently captured unsold. He's mute but, as you can see, strongly built. He'd make a fine farmhand, or perhaps a pleasure slave."

*Pleasure slave? She didn't mention that.*

The bald Svartr, looking regal and impatient, gestures for her to get on with it.

The gray-robed Svartr, apparently the auctioneer, nods and speaks in a formal tone. "The city starts the bidding at one hundred merker."

*What the hell is a merker? It'd be nice to know what I'm worth.*

The bald Svartr nods.

The auctioneer smiles thankfully and continues. "Do I hear a bid of one hundred and twenty-five for this well-muscled unsold?"

One of the litter slaves stands with his ear pressed to the velvet canopy, receiving instructions from within. He raises his hand and speaks. "Three hundred merker."

The auctioneer bows, excited. *I bet she gets a piece of the sale.*

The bald Svartr scowls, clenching her clockwork hand. I wonder if there's personal history between these two buyers.

The auctioneer speaks softly now, afraid to push her luck. "We have a generous bid of three hundred merker. Do I hear three hundred and twenty-five?"

The bald Svartr fumes but doesn't bid.

The auctioneer gives a long look to each buyer. "We have a bid of three hundred merker. Going once, going twice …"

The bald Svartr makes an angry gesture. "Three hundred and twenty-five."

*I've decided I don't want her to win. She'll blame me for overpaying. Better if I go to the mystery buyer.*

The auctioneer turns to the canopied litter. "We have three hundred and twenty-five. Do I hear three hundred and fifty?"

Silence from the dark canopy.

*Shit, the mystery buyer hit their limit.*

"We have a bid of three hundred and twenty-five. Going once, going twice …"

The litter slave raises his hand again. "We request a personal inspection."

The bald Svartr rolls her eyes and huffs.

The auctioneer steps aside. "Of course, as you wish."

The velvet parts and a figure emerges from the canopy: a short female in a black veil and robes. A dark elf!

This is the first Fae I've seen since coming to Dragonworks. I wonder where they're hiding.

Moving gracefully, she ascends the stairs and emerges on stage.

As she approaches, I notice her spicy scent.

She stands before me, a little under five foot tall. I see big amber eyes behind her veil.

She slips off a black glove, exposing a delicate hand. She has smooth, dark skin with a purple hue.

She makes a soft, shushing sound. Is she warning me not to speak, or trying to calm me?

Her hand extends slowly, cautiously, as if she's approaching a wild animal. She rests her palm against my chest. Her touch is soft and warm.

Suddenly, the world disappears.

I see the dark elf before me, her hand on my chest, but the stage looks faded and indistinct. The auctioneer and the bald Svartr appear as wraiths, moving around at impossible speeds.

I suddenly realize what's happened. This dark elf has taken me to Som, a reflective plane used by Fae and witches.

She stole me from the auction!

# Breeding Program

### ASH KINLEY

My heart pounds in shock. In a matter of seconds, two sentinels have pulled Stefan and Tyler into their mouths, and now the horrible creatures are slipping into the sewers with their catches.

*Oh my God, are they being killed? Are the toads eating them?*

I feel a wave of nausea and despair as tears flood my eyes. What just happened? What gave us away?

I run toward the open manhole cover where the toads disappeared. Already, the cover is closing.

I leap toward the hole.

But I never reach it.

Something hits me hard in midair.

I smack to the ground, tangled up with the invoked Svartr who tackled me. She smells musky and I feel her growl reverberating in my body.

My first instinct is to invoke Seeker and attack. But in my peripheral vision, I see more Svartr approaching, all with

faecast rifles. If I fight now, I will die, and more importantly, Seeker will die. I can't let that happen.

I go limp in the Svartr's arms. I'm relieved when she
doesn't bite or scratch me.

A curious crowd of slaves gathers round as several Svartr
haul me to my feet.

I scratch the skin over my heart with my index finger just
before the Svartr secure my hands with faecast cuffs. I hope
my message got out to one of the slaves in the crowd.

The Svartr who tackled me, a huge woman with a pock-
marked face, looks pleased with herself as she checks the
inside of my lower lip.

Her forehead wrinkles. "Unsold? How can that be?"

My head covering has fallen off, and the Svartr tugs at
my hair. "No matter. You're a red. I'll probably get a bonus."

An old female Svartr approaches, wearing a brown robe
with a white belt. One of her eyes is covered with a patch.
The white scars on either side of the patch suggest the eye
was lost in some long-ago battle.

She checks my lip and frowns. "Where are you from, girl?"

I'm relieved they don't seem to know who I am. Time to
give my cover story.

"I'm from the tanning district."

The one-eyed Svartr laughs. "Your teeth are too good
for that. Besides, a red like you would've been grabbed up
long ago."

She takes my mirror and pouch. My time compass and
gate stones are in the pouch, but I have bigger worries
now. What happened to Stefan? Is he still alive? Somehow,

I feel like I'd know if he died, that something would die inside me too.

The group of Svartr lead me out of the Servant Quarter and into a more secure area with checkpoints and gated streets. There are fewer slaves here, and more of the older, robed Svartr. It's strange seeing Svartr past their prime, who aren't outfitted for battle.

The one-eyed Svartr leads me into a building made of the thick brown plastic I've seen everywhere. I'm expecting a prison, but it's actually nice in here. There's a water fountain and a rock garden filled with stones that glow blue and green. There's also a faint odor that smells like condensed milk.

I'm led to a room with a tub of steaming water. They leave me to bathe while a pair of armed guards wait outside. The bathwater is slick with an oil that smells like flowers.

This seemingly kind treatment doesn't give me comfort. Do they want their slave cleaned for sale? I fight off a surge of panic.

After I wash up, a Svartr girl with a slight smile brings me a robe to wear. It's soft and purple and ties with a white belt. My sandals have been replaced by fur-lined slippers that tickle my feet.

The girl leads me to another room where the one-eyed Svartr sits behind a desk, sipping something sharp-smelling from a brown plastic cup as she uses a faecast pen to make notations in a leather journal.

She gestures for me to take the seat across from her, but I remain standing. My fear is turning to anger. I want to know what happened to Stefan and Tyler, but I'm not sure I should ask. If they're still alive, would my questions put them in danger? It doesn't seem like the Svartr know who I really am. I have to find some way to use that to my advantage.

Something's been bothering me and I finally realize what it is. Why haven't the Svartr realized I'm Were? The Svartr are Were, and we can sense our own kind. Is Skadi protecting me somehow? Or maybe these Svartr have changed over the last thousand years, and no longer have that awareness.

The one-eyed Svartr sighs when she sees that I've remained standing.

"Suit yourself. This won't take long. I have news for you, slave. You have been selected to participate in the city breeding program, an opportunity most slaves would kill for. Reds like you breed like rabbits, so I'm certain you'll fit in well."

*Breeding program?*

She takes another sip of her drink. "Our operations at this center are fairly standard. All copulations are scheduled and observed. Your first two children belong to the city. If you produce a third child, you are allowed to raise that child to the age of sixteen, after which the child is assigned a slave caste in the city or sold as a servant to a private buyer. Production of a third child also entitles you to a husband, should you choose to take one. If you fail to produce a third child within your fertile years, you'll be sent to the nursery, where the darkling young will bleed the life from you. Any questions?"

For some reason, I start to laugh. This is all so ridiculous, like something from a horror movie. Any moment now, I'm expecting to wake up and look back on this as the wildest nightmare of my life.

Reflexively, I glance back at the door. Sadly, there's no chance of escape. A pair of steely-eyed Svartr watch me, guns at the ready.

The one-eyed Svartr, annoyed by my laughter, makes a dismissive gesture, and the guards lead me out of her office.

They take me down the hallway and place me in a line with three other numb-faced female slaves in robes like mine. One of them has red hair. None of them make eye contact.

At the front of the line is a door with only the top half open. A middle-aged Svartr dispenses a large plastic cup to each woman in turn. She waits for the slave to drink the contents, then takes the empty cup and motions the next slave forward.

When I reach the front of the line, she hands me a cup. It feels warm in my hand. The liquid inside is brown and chunky. It's the source of the condensed milk smell that I noticed before.

My stomach flips as I stare at the drink. I can't help but ask, "What is it?"

The woman looks annoyed. "Your fertility drink. Swallow it down, all of it, or we'll force it into you."

As much as I want to toss the drink in her face, it's smarter for me to play the good prisoner until I have a chance to escape. I need to get out of here, contact Thora, and find out what happened to Stefan and Tyler.

I hold my nose and swallow the disgusting liquid. It leaves a sickly-sweet taste in my mouth.

The guards escort me deeper into the building. The hallways are lit by glowing glass globes. All the doors are closed. The walls are empty, but at each intersection I see a strange circle in the floor, filled with lichens and glowing mosses of many colors. Is it supposed to be art?

As we pass one room, I hear a couple having sex.

The guards finally stop at a door engraved with Fae symbols representing a room number.

I can read the symbols, thanks to Skadi's gift of tongues. This is room thirty-six. The guards push me inside.

A human slave, a woman in a yellow robe with a white belt, stands and approaches me with a sympathetic smile. She's in her midtwenties, very pregnant, and gives me an awkward hug. "My name is Sabra. I'll be your mentor here."

I don't hug her back. Her swollen belly feels like a threat.

I scan the room. It's small, with a bed and a circular wooden table with two chairs.

One odd thing catches my eye: a black curtain on the wall, with a single chair facing the curtain. Is there a window there?

The guards move outside the room and close the door behind them. Sabra leads me to the curtain and gestures for me to sit in the chair.

"Your new mate will arrive soon. His room is connected to yours through this portal. In a few minutes, he will draw the curtain, and he'll be sitting on the other side. For the first ten days, neither of you is allowed to cross the portal, but you may sit in the chairs and converse. Spend these days getting to know him, and then they'll schedule your first session."

For one crazy moment, I find myself praying that Stefan will be on the other side of that curtain. He has to be alive, right? I would know if he was dead.

My mentor squeezes my hand. "I have to go now, Ash. Enjoy your conversation. Please don't try to leave, there are guards outside your door."

My body tenses and I feel a surge of adrenaline. She used my name! I never told anyone my name.

I open my mouth to speak but she puts a finger over my lips. "It will be all right, Ash. They picked someone special for you."

She hurries out of the room, and I hear the door lock behind her.

*Someone special? What does that mean?*

I hear someone move behind the curtain and I spring from my seat.

*Who the hell is on the other side?*

Suddenly, the curtain parts, and I see a small female dark elf in black robes and a dark veil.

I feel my heart thumping. They know who I really am! They've known all along.

I never had a chance.

# TEMPLE OF MIRRORS

## TYLER BUCK

THE THREE DARK ELVES keep their rifles pointed at me, saying nothing. My options at this point are limited. I'm not rested enough for a time jump, and there's no room in this cellar to shift into dragon form.

What do these Fae want? Why are they just standing there?

For some reason, I feel like needling them. "If you're supposed to be a firing squad, you suck at it."

None of them reacts.

Now that my eyes are adjusted to the dim light, I see they don't have their fingers on the triggers. That's a good sign. Also, my timesight isn't kicking in, so I don't think any violence is about to happen.

I wonder what they'd do if I went up the stairs, pounded on the trapdoor, and asked Valda to let me out.

Suddenly, two figures appear out of nowhere. It's Stefan, shirtless, hand in hand with a dark elf. Wow, they must have blipped in from Som!

Stefan smiles, breaking away from the dark Fae. We share a handshake and one-armed dude hug.

He squeezes my shoulder. "Glad you made it. How'd you get out of the sentinel's mouth? Time shift?"

I nod. "What about you?"

"I went along for the ride. Then they tried to sell me as a slave and my Fae friend jacked me from the auction."

"Friend?"

Two more figures suddenly appear. It's Ash, holding hands with another veiled dark elf.

Ash leaves the elf and flies across the room into Stefan's arms. They laugh, and Ash cries, and they whisper things to each other.

Then Ash gives me a teary hug as well. "I'm so happy you're alive, Tyler!"

"You too."

Stefan approaches and Ash jumps back into his arms.

As they kiss, I can't help thinking Stefan is getting the better greeting. It makes me wonder where Rosemarie is right now. Does she still think about me? If we were reunited right now, would she be crying tears of joy, like Ash? I'm glad that Stefan and Ash have each other, but I can't help feeling a little sorry for myself.

The three elves with the rifles lower their weapons, and another dark Fae appears out of Som. This one is stooped with age and wears a veil made of thin metallic links chained together into a semi-sheer fabric. All the other dark elves in the room take a knee and bow their heads to her. She gestures for them to rise.

I'm guessing she's the queen bee. For some reason, she addresses me, rather than Stefan and Ash.

"Young dragon, I understand you're looking for Thora."

I don't respond. These people *seem* friendly, and must be part of the resistance, but still, they're freaking dark elves and I've seen how they feed their young.

The queen bee continues. "I apologize for your rude reception. We've hidden your presence from Sindri, but it seems one of the sentinels detected your high body heat. The others got taken because they were with you. We're relieved you're all safe now. Some introductions are in order. First of all, you should know there is no Thora. She's something created to distract the loyalists. I'm afraid you will have to settle for me. My name is Sun Dreamer. I am the great-granddaughter of Sun Walker."

Ash steps up, her voice taut. "I know that name. She worked for Gríma."

Sun Dreamer nods. "It would be more accurate to say she worked *with* Gríma, for a short time. It might interest you to know that in the years following, Sun Walker rebelled against Sindri and was killed by him. Before she died, she wrote about you three, speculating you would reappear one day. I have been waiting. The resistance has been waiting."

Ash looks skeptical. "Why did Sun Walker turn on Sindri?"

"Because he broke our covenant with nature. His only concerns are his forges and machines. Look what he's done to the world above. Sun Walker knew this destruction would come, and she died trying to stop it. Over the years, many rebellions have risen and fallen. But this time, some of the Svartr are willing to join us, and most importantly, we have you three."

Stefan's about to speak, but Sun Dreamer raises her hand, as if anticipating his words.

"I understand your distrust of us. You haven't been here long enough to distinguish friend from foe. So, allow me to make the first gesture of peace. Actually, it would be the second gesture. The first gesture was bringing you all together."

Sun Dreamer signals to the dark elves, and they lay their rifles on the ground.

Another dark elf pops in from Som and returns Ash's pouch to her.

*That's a relief. I hope the gate stones are still in there.*

Ash checks inside her pouch, then smiles.

From under her veil, Sun Dreamer makes a surprisingly loud whistle.

Valda descends from the trapdoor and returns my faecast rifle and folded space pouch to me. I look into the pouch. It's too full of crap to inventory, but I'm guessing it's all there. Nice to have my crystal claws and crash cube with me again. And then, of course, there's the Devourer.

I take the pair of faecast rifles from the pouch and give them to Ash and Stefan.

Stefan addresses Sun Dreamer, his voice flat. "Tell us how to find Sindri."

She turns to him. "If you plan to kill him, be advised that may prove difficult. He abandoned his flesh long ago. He has a clockwork body now, fashioned after his own."

Ash looks worried. "Does he still have blood?"

*I'm wondering the same thing.*

Sun Dreamer faces Ash. "Interesting question, why do you ask?"

"We're not here to kill his body, we're here to kill his soul. We have the Devourer."

Sun Dreamer stiffens and remains silent for a few moments.

At some unspoken signal, all the dark elves, except for Sun Dreamer, disappear into Som.

Stefan positions his back against the cellar wall, ready for trouble.

I can't see Sun Dreamer's face, but I can imagine why she's upset. We discussed this problem in an ethics class at the Academy.

Sun Dreamer speaks to Ash, her voice soft. "I think I understand your plan. The soul is eternal, so if it's destroyed, it will be as if Sindri never existed, and all the harm he did will disappear. But you see, my people and I will probably disappear as well."

Ash looks taken aback, so I speak up.

"Sun Dreamer, I've studied this issue. Dimensional theory says that your bodies exist, and will continue to exist, in alternate timelines where we never arrived to challenge Sindri, or in timelines where we failed to stop him. Many theoreticians believe, and I think correctly, that while you have many bodies, you have but one soul, a soul that is multidimensional and continues to live on in *all* of your many Sun Dreamer bodies. A correction in this timeline will not destroy that soul."

She sighs. "What a lovely piece of sophistry. It's scant solace, but I suppose it will have to do."

We all sit around a stone table in the rebel war room, a bubble chamber in the solid rock, accessible only via Som.

Sun Dreamer stands at the head of the table. As she speaks, she uses glamour to project images directly into our heads.

"The majority of our people live in the lowest levels of Dragonworks."

In my mind, I see muscular dark elf males, soaked in sweat, pouring lava into glowing cauldrons. There are hundreds of them. Thousands.

"We outnumber the humans and Svartr almost ten to one. Most Dökkálfar are loyalists, of course, but we do have several hundred sympathizers available to us at any time."

Stefan raises his hand. "How many Svartr and humans on our side?"

"Nearly four hundred human slaves, and perhaps thirty Svartr. The Svartr hate Sindri, so we ought to have more of them, but they loathe working with resistance slaves. Of those thirty Svartr, only seven can fight. The rest are feeling their years. We can get guns into the hands of everyone. We have more guns than people."

Stefan looks wary. "You have a lot of help. If taking out Sindri is doable, why hasn't the resistance done it already?"

Sun Dreamer takes a seat and steeples her gloved hands. "Two reasons. First, there is an obstacle we've yet to overcome, and I'll speak of it shortly. Second, there's a prevailing sense that we can't win, that Sindri is too strong. But your arrival has tipped the balance, and our people are ready to make their move."

Stefan presses her. "Talk more about the obstacle."

She stands, seemingly annoyed. "Sindri's workshop isn't in Dragonworks. It's at his palace in the extraplanar world of Svartalfheim."

Sun Dreamer projects another glamour illusion, and I see a palace with gold walls covered with sparkling gems.

She continues her guided tour. "This part of Svartalfheim has no entryways and is protected against travel from Som and Velox. It is linked to a place here in the city, the Temple of Mirrors ..."

In her glamour, I see an octagonal faecast structure, the walls inscribed with cryptic runes and symbols.

"This is the outer sanctum, where the court elite come to worship the idols of Sindri and Mirror Gríma. There are smaller versions of this temple scattered around the city, but this one is the finest."

I see faecast pews covered with cushions. The walls and ceiling are decorated with colorful mosses forming geometric patterns. At the front are clockwork statues of Sindri and Mirror Gríma, standing side by side, both about five feet tall.

I note one disappointing fact about the temple. The walls aren't high enough to accommodate my dragon form. If I go inside, I'll have to fight as a human.

Sun Dreamer continues her discussion of the temple. "There is also an inner sanctum. I cannot show it to you, because I've never seen it. It is said to have eight walls, covered with mirrors. Here is where Sindri and clock-work Gríma meet with the court elite. Sindri is only there on occasion, but clockwork Gríma guards the sanctum at all times."

Confused, I raise my hand. "I thought Mirror Gríma wasn't a physical presence, that she was confined to mirrors."

Sun Dreamer nods. "Yes, but she also has a clockwork body, as does Sindri. I know of no way to destroy Mirror Gríma, but with Sindri, there may be a way. Though he has no blood in his clockwork body, he keeps one last vestige of his former flesh. He stores his heart in a box. There is still blood in his heart, and if you can open the box, you can use the Devourer to destroy Sindri's soul."

Stefan nods warily. "What's the catch? You need a special key to get into this box?"

Sun Dreamer shakes her head. "The box has no lock, no opening, and it cannot be destroyed by any force on this earth, save one. Mirror Gríma's clockwork body, the one in the inner sanctum, carries a gold sword called Tyrfing. It's a cursed weapon that must take a life when it's drawn. But it can cut through anything, including Sindri's box."

Stefan nods. "I know how to use a sword, just tell us where to find the box."

*It's a cursed sword, Stefan! Did you hear that part?*

"Sindri keeps the box in his palace. I'm not sure where. But there is no better time to be searching. Sindri is living in his workshop beneath the palace, obsessed with his clockwork dragon. He is distracted. His guard will be down."

*If the workshop is big enough for a clockwork dragon, it may have room for my dragon form.*

Sun Dreamer leans forward, her voice intense. "Breach the inner sanctum of the Temple of Mirrors, kill clockwork Gríma and take her sword. Then travel to Svartalfheim, infiltrate Sindri's palace, and find his heart box. Use Tyrfing to cut open the box, and then destroy Sindri's soul with the Devourer."

*I'm gonna need you to write all that down.*

Stefan frowns. "This plan has a lot of moving parts. How well guarded is the temple?"

"Four to six armed Svartr on the temple grounds. Another four in the outer sanctum. We don't know how the inner sanctum is protected."

"With your numbers, it sounds like you could easily overrun the place."

"Sadly, no. There's a rumor that our faecast rifles won't function in the inner sanctum, so resistance fighters are unwilling to go there."

"Which fighters, exactly? The dark elves?"

"Especially the Dökkálfar. The inner sanctum is proofed against travel via Som or Velox. My people never go anywhere without an available escape route."

Stefan, annoyed, cracks a knuckle. "Can we at least use resistance fighters to clear a path to the inner sanctum, and then prevent reinforcements from arriving?"

She nods. "Certainly."

"One more question. If the Fae guns don't work in there, how do we kill clockwork Gríma?"

Sun Dreamer pauses, sitting back in her chair. "That's an excellent question. I wish I had an excellent answer. I can tell you that her parts are made of sindrion, immune to normal weapons, as well as the claws and fangs of the Were. She is also immune to our Fae abilities."

Stefan shakes his head. "I'm starting to see why you've never tried this before."

I raise my hand. "I'll kill clockwork Gríma, if you like."

All eyes turn toward me. I suppose I owe them an explanation.

"I'll have to fight in human form, but my crystal claws will cut into sindrion. I used them to break a faecast chain."

Stefan tilts his head respectfully. "Thank you, Tyler, we'll take you up on that offer."

Ash smiles, but I can see her concern for me.

*Have I bitten off more than I can chew?*

Sun Dreamer stands, her arms braced on the table. "This is a promising approach, but there is still the obstacle I mentioned. There are no entryways into Svartalfheim, where Sindri's palace lies. It is only accessible via crossplanar travel. We don't know how he's making that trip. That journey is beyond our capabilities."

Ash springs to her feet, eager to make a contribution. She scatters her gate stones across the table. "Show me how to spell Svartalfheim using Norse runes."

We rest a day so I'll be able to make a time jump if needed in an emergency. In the meantime, we receive good food and a new set of clothing.

Stefan uses the extra time to modify the captured body armor so that he, Ash, and I are well protected.

Fae guns might not work in the inner sanctum, but fortunately, we brought our own conventional arms. Ash carries the assault rifle she captured from Gríma's soldiers at the Jotunborg, as well as her slingshot, and Stefan has his Glock and a faecast dagger. I take the scope off my hunting revolver and strap the big gun to my hip.

Stefan gives us some tactical training on how to enter a room as a team, without shooting each other. At times, Ash is a little moony-eyed over Stefan, but he has infinite patience with her. I just hope they can focus once we get there.

As annoyed as I am by their new smoochiness, I realize I'm just a jealous fool. I had that feeling once with Rosemarie, and I vow to have it again.

I'm normally jumpy before a big operation, but not this time. I think that's because I'm so tired, and still not recovered from the metaphysician's chop shop. Even rested, I don't really trust myself to make a big jump quickly and accurately, but a small jump might be enough to save our asses.

Soon, it's *go time*, and we gather in a vast underground staging area to prepare our assault. Hundreds of dark elves are here to take our human and Svartr forces to the Temple of Mirrors via Som. The plan is to pop into the outer sanctum and temple grounds, take the guards out by surprise, and secure the area against reinforcements.

From there, the dark elves will use their tunneling magic to breach the door between the outer and inner sanctum, where Stefan, Ash, and I will do our thing. Hopefully I can kill clockwork Gríma quickly, Stefan can grab her magic sword, and Ash can transport us into Sindri's palace.

The more I think about it, the more I'm liking our chances. We have two werewolves and a time-traveling dracoform, all heavily armed and armored.

We got this.

# Last Act of Kindness

## Ash Kinley

THE HIKE THROUGH SOM takes hours. For every twenty or thirty steps we take, we cover only a single step in the real world. In the beginning, we walk through solid rock, led by our dark Fae guides until eventually, we reach the city near the Temple of Mirrors.

The city looks black and white, as if seen through a shroud. It's deathly quiet. People pass through the streets at a ridiculous pace, like a sped-up video. I'm feeling queasy, and I'm eager to return to the real world, or Mortalos, as Sun Dreamer calls it.

The octagonal temple looks exactly how Sun Dreamer showed it, though its green metallic walls appear gray from inside Som.

A couple hundred rebel slaves, all armed with faecast rifles, position themselves around the outside of the temple. When they jump back into the real world, the Svartr temple guards won't stand a chance.

Another two hundred slaves, plus seven rebel Svartr, continue straight through the walls of the temple. Passing through objects takes concentration, but I got plenty of practice when we were hiking through solid rock. The thin wall around the temple only feels like a speed bump.

I look ahead at Stefan and Tyler. We've already spoken our final words before the mission. I can't even remember what stupid things I said. Somehow, *good luck* doesn't really cut it.

I'm so worried about Stefan. He's really brave, and he likes to shoulder the biggest risks. If something goes wrong in there, he won't hesitate to sacrifice himself, and he's not gonna ask for permission first.

I want this terrible mission to be over. I want to be back in Corby, sitting safe with Stefan, enjoying that dinner we never got to have.

The outer sanctum seems much bigger than what Sun Dreamer showed us. There's space in these pews for hundreds, if not thousands of worshippers. The colorful mosses on the ceiling now glow in shades of gray, but the patterns are no less striking. One has eyes that seem to watch me.

The two hundred human slaves, along with five Svartr, position themselves around the outer sanctum where there are guards or doors.

The rest of us join Sun Dreamer's dark elf demolition team at the entrance to the inner sanctum, a star-shaped grillwork of faecast bars. I can't even imagine how that gate opens. There isn't a handle. This is as far as we can go, since the inner sanctum is barred from entry via Som.

Two rebel Svartr, breaking ranks with the others, have joined us at the gate to the inner sanctum. They wear black combat armor and carry faecast rifles with bayonets. They've heard that their rifles may not work in the inner sanctum, so they both carry wicked faecast knives as backup. I'm glad that these two, at least, decided to help us. So together with the Svartr, that makes five of us who'll be assaulting the inner sanctum.

On Sun Dreamer's signal, all of the Were, except for Tyler, invoke.

It feels good to invoke. It's reassuring to have Seeker with me now.

Our Fae guides jump us into the real world, drop us off, and then jump back into Som. My stomach flips, and the sudden riot of color hurts my eyes.

I hear gunfire as the resistance fighters take down the temple guards.

As the dark Fae work on the gate, I stare at the golden idols of Sindri and Gríma at the front of the temple. At any moment, I expect them to come to life.

Gripping my rifle tight, I look over at Stefan. But he doesn't return my gaze. He's busy scanning the area and assessing threats. I'm a little jealous that he can ignore me so easily, but I understand. This is life or death.

Tyler, however, seeks out my eyes and shares a smile. He's wearing his crystal claws and looks relaxed and confident. How can he do that? I don't feel nearly so comfortable. The whole scene has a surreal quality, like it's happening to another person.

There's a sharp cracking sound and I jerk. The stone floor below the gate has collapsed, leaving the gate hanging ajar. All the dark elves have jumped into Som.

Stefan calls out as he motions us forward, "Don't look in the mirrors."

Stefan is first through the gap, followed by Tyler, then me. The two grim-faced Svartr women, both of them my age, follow me. We all hold our guns at the ready.

We enter a wide octagonal inner chamber over a hundred feet across, with huge mirrors for walls. In the center of the room stands a pile of treasure taller than me. I see gold coins, gold bars, gold jewelry, and gold objects such as small statues, vases, cups, and utensils. Light from glowing spheres in the ceiling reflects off the gold, hurting my eyes.

We're alone here. No sign of clockwork Gríma.

Stefan calls out, "Shoot out the mirrors, but don't look into them."

But as he finishes speaking, all hell breaks loose.

Six figures step out from inside each of the eight mirrors, and suddenly the chamber is holding around fifty people.

One of the six figures is someone I expected. It's clockwork Gríma, a black-masked mechanical monstrosity about eight feet tall. Her green faecast body is built like a tank. Steam drifts from her ears as her legs pump and her gears grind. Her red eyes stare at me as she draws a sword from a scabbard at her metal hip.

The sword must be Tyrfing. I hear a distant rumble as it's drawn. The hilt is made of gold, and the blade, a searing length of fiery lava, is nearly three feet long.

My heart pounds as I see *eight* of these clockwork Grímas, all carrying that same terrifying sword.

But she is just one of the figures that step through the mirrors. There are also eight new Stefans, eight new Tylers, eight new copies of each Svartr, and eight new Ashes.

Reacting quickly, Stefan is the first to fire. He shoots out two of the mirrors as the Grímas rush us. But breaking the mirrors has no effect on them.

I fire on the nearest clockwork Gríma, as does Tyler. The Svartr also fire their weapons, proving that faecast rifles actually do work in the inner sanctum.

Another mirror breaks, but none of the Grímas go down, and now they're among us.

I step back, dropping my rifle as a clockwork Gríma swings Tyrfing at me. The blade misses my neck by inches. My heart pounds as I realize how close I am to death.

Since my bullets didn't work against her, I'm forced to use Seeker's claws, and I'm not optimistic about my chances. This is really a job for Tyler's crystal claws, but he's already busy fighting a pair of clockwork Grímas.

I'll have to deal with this one on my own. I do have one thing going for me. With Seeker invoked, I'm faster than clockwork Gríma. I need to use that to my advantage.

As Gríma draws Tyrfing back for another strike, I dart forward, my left hand reaching up to pin back her right arm, and my right-hand claws aiming for her red eyes.

I'm stunned when I stumble through her without making contact. She's isn't real, she's an illusion!

I take a quick glance around at the chaotic scene. The copies of Stefan, Tyler, the Svartr and myself, are all fighting with clockwork Grímas. I can't tell who are my real friends, and who are illusions.

Suddenly, nine Svartr fall, their heads rolling away in a cloud of inky smoke, filling the room with a burnt flesh smell. It seems that one of the Svartr died, and so did all of her copies. Somewhere in here, the real clockwork Gríma, with the real Tyrfing, is killing us. But which one? How do I get the real Gríma to reveal herself?

Ignoring the phantom Gríma I'm fighting, I run to the middle of the room and grab a gold bar from the treasure pile. I hold it high and yell, "It's mine now!"

One of the Grímas suddenly snaps her head around, her red eyes glowing, and makes a beeline for me. This is the real clockwork Gríma, with the real Tyrfing!

I point at her and yell, "Tyler, she's the real one."

The eight other versions of me also point at Gríma and shout the same thing at the same time.

But all nine Tylers are gathered at one of the remaining mirrors, staring at Mirror Gríma's huge, metallic face. She's speaking to them through the mirror, but I can't hear what she's saying.

The other Svartr is dead now too, lying on the floor with a missing leg. Her eight copies also lie on the floor.

The copies of me and Stefan are all busy fighting illusionary Grímas, all except for one Stefan, the real Stefan, who grabs for a faecast rifle lying on the floor. But his hands pass through the rifle. It too, is an illusion, so he scrambles to grab another one.

I feel the heat from Tyrfing before Gríma reaches me. I scramble up the mountain of treasure, trying to distract her, buying time for Stefan to find a real rifle.

Clockwork Gríma, disgusted by my desecration of her treasure, howls with fury. The other Grímas also howl. The sound cracks another mirror. I cover my ears to stop my skull from splitting.

The treasure mountain suddenly collapses beneath me. As I fall, clockwork Gríma lunges forward. Tyrfing jabs toward my heart like a spear.

Time seems to slow, and a sick realization hits me. Gríma is going to stab me with that sword! Sure, I've got body armor, but Sun Dreamer said Tyrfing can cut through anything, and looking at the brutal weapon, I believe it.

When the sword hits me, Seeker will be the first to die, and then me. Even if I survive by some wild luck, Seeker surely won't. Before I feel the stab of the sword, I feel a stab of fear for my wolf. The majestic creature who gave me a new life is about to die.

I can't let that happen!

Before the sword reaches me, I uninvoke. Let it be my last act of kindness. As Seeker leaves my body, I whisper a goodbye to her.

At the last moment, I manage to lift a gold platter as a shield, but the hot sword plunges through it like butter, its molten blade piercing my heart.

Gríma's head disintegrates as faecast bullets tear into her from behind. She releases the hilt of Tyrfing and the blade grows dim and cold. I look at the weapon lodged in my chest, knowing I have only seconds to live.

It doesn't hurt as much as I imagined. But the pain will be terrible for Stefan. This will devastate him. I wish I could tell him I'm sorry. I wish I could tell him goodbye, but the room is already spinning into darkness.

I scream in grief, horror, and frustration, but no sound escapes my lips. I'm not ready to leave this world. I will miss Stefan, my poor lost dogs, and the stars in the night sky.

I see Skadi now, a sad look on her face, coming to take me to the afterworld. Which world will it be? Helheim? Will I spend an eternity helping my alcoholic mother make moonshine?

I'm a good person. I didn't deserve this fate. How could the world be so cruel?

Skadi reaches for my hand, but her face is hidden by the veil of my tears.

## LOVE IS A DUTY

### STEFAN HILDEBRAND

As I LIFT the faecast rifle to fire at clockwork Gríma, I see Ash is down. What happened? A moment ago, she was on her feet, in control, buying me time to get the rifle.

Fear explodes inside me as I shoot Gríma in the head. Fear for Ash. An intense fear I've never felt before. Something terrible has happened.

As Gríma's mechanical head breaks apart, the phantom people in the chamber all disappear.

I sprint toward Ash and I see something my mind can't comprehend.

Tyrfing, now released by Gríma, juts from Ash's chest. The sword no longer burns, but the weapon has pierced her heart. Her kind, sweet heart.

I feel pain in my chest as I kneel beside her. I can't breathe. Am I having a heart attack?

Ash's face is peaceful, her fingers outstretched as if reaching for something.

She isn't breathing, and of course she has no pulse. The sword left a charred wreck where her heart should be.

I get tunnel vision and have to force air into my lungs.

I uninvoke. As Defender leaves, I feel a wave of horror rush through me. Fighting the urge to vomit, I reach out and stroke Ash's pale, soft cheek.

"I'm sorry I couldn't stop Gríma in time. I'm so sorry."

The world blurs as tears fill my eyes. I fall down beside Ash, cupping her head and resting it gently against mine.

Something shifts inside me. Nothing seems important anymore. Not Corby, not the damaged timeline, and definitely not this fucking mission. None of it means anything if Ash is dead.

Tears roll down my cheeks as I whisper in her ear. "This can't be real. I love you. We were going to be together. This wasn't supposed to happen. This can't happen."

Suddenly, the headless clockwork Gríma stirs to life. Her mechanical hand reaches out, grabbing blindly for the hilt of the sword lodged in Ash's chest.

I hear myself screaming as I grab the hilt and pull the sword from Ash's body. The weapon leaps to life, blade shifting orange and white, like hot plasma.

I'm going to kill now. I will kill and kill, until I die. I want to die. I want to be with Ash.

Tyrfing cuts through Gríma like a knife through a cake. I laugh in grim satisfaction as her sparking gears grind and her hissing pumps spew steam. Soon, the room smells like ozone, and clockwork Gríma lies in smoldering pieces at my feet.

"Don't worry, Stefan. If you like, we can make a clockwork Ash."

I turn to the voice, coming from one of the unbroken mirrors. Gríma's metallic face smiles at me.

I know I'm not supposed to look into the mirrors, but I don't fucking care.

I run to the mirror, raising the sword to strike.

Mirror Gríma yells, "Stop! I command you."

I can't stop laughing as I swing the sword, shattering the mirror and cutting through the sindrion wall behind it.

I see Gríma's fractured face in a large shard of mirror on the floor. Her eyes are wide in disbelief. "You will obey me, as all others have done. You're no exception, Stefan Hildebrand. Abandon your rage and obey me!"

I break the mirror shard with the sword. The weapon moves fluidly in my hand, as if it's been there all my life.

Looking around, I see there's one last mirror still intact. Tyler stands stupidly before it, mesmerized by an image of Gríma. I shove him aside and break the mirror.

I spin to confront Tyler. "*You* were supposed to fight Gríma. Not Ash. You! I told you not to look in the mirror."

He responds, still in a daze. "I didn't. Not at first. I just heard her voice."

I scream at him, "Liar!"

I lift Tyrfing to strike Tyler, but suddenly hear a soft voice by the entrance to the sanctum.

"He's probably telling the truth."

I whirl to see Sun Dreamer standing on the threshold, unwilling to enter the chamber.

She speaks from behind her chain mesh veil. "The less human you are, and the more powerful, the more you are vulnerable to mirror magic. It is a paradoxical magic created by the ancients. In this case, I suspect Tyler's dragon was his weakness."

I feel my adrenaline level dip as I'm forced to process Sun Dreamer's words. I need to calm down and think. Killing Tyler would be stupid. I *need* him.

I grab him by the shoulder, directing the hot sword away from him. "Tyler, you have to go back."

He still looks dazed. "What?"

"You have to go back in time, to save Ash."

"Save her?"

I can't help screaming at him, "She's dead, Tyler!"

He looks around, panic stricken, and sees Ash lying on the mound of treasure. "Oh no!"

He stumbles over to her, body swaying like a drunk.

His trembling hand passes over the charred hole in her chest. "I have a first aid kit! I can help her."

I sprint over and kick him. He tumbles down the side of the gold heap, then crouches against a mirrorless wall, drawing his knees to his face to cover his tears.

I want to hit him, but I force myself to speak. "A first aid kit isn't gonna cut it. You need to go back in time and stop her from coming here."

He gets to his feet and wipes his face with his sleeve. "I want to help, but I'm not sure how. If I go back in time and inadvertently make contact with my past self, it would cause a temporal anomaly that might prevent us from repairing this timeline and returning home. I'd have to go back to a time where Ash and I were separated. But then how do I find her? And even if I could, you think I could stop her from going on this mission? You know her, Stefan, she's as bad as you."

My face clenches and my tunnel vision returns. "Are you saying you won't help?"

Tyler spreads his arms in a gesture of peace. "I'm saying I want to help. But it's not that simple. If it was doable, I would have already done it, and Ash would have already been saved. But I didn't show up to stop her, so that means I couldn't. Do you understand?"

My head spins and a red haze covers my eyes. "You *will* go back! You have to go back!"

A tired voice speaks from behind me. "Stefan, put the sword down."

I know that voice. It's a voice I feared I'd never hear again.

I turn slowly, afraid I'll discover that it's my imagination.

It's Ash! It's really her. She's standing before me, looking tired and worried, and without the chest wound!

The sword drops from my hand and I run to her. As we embrace, I realize she's no illusion. She's warm, and real, and smells like Ash.

My throat knots, and I can't speak.

Tyler approaches and hugs her from the other side. "I'm so sorry, Ash. I let you down."

She shakes her head. "Neither of you let me down. We all did the best we could."

I smile at her through a blur of tears and trace her face with my fingertips. "I thought I'd lost you."

She shakes her head and kisses me fiercely. "You'll never lose me. We'll always be together, in this world or the next."

But Ash isn't smiling. She looks sad.

I look deep into her eyes. "What's wrong?"

She bites her lip and takes my hand, drawing me to the place where she fell in battle.

Another body lies there now, an elderly female giant with long white braids.

Ash crouches next to her, squeezing her lifeless hand. "This is Skadi. She traded her life for mine. I tried to stop her, but she said she was tired, and ready to join the Old Gods in Valhalla."

Ash's tears splash down on Skadi, twinkling with light as they hit her wrinkled skin.

I kneel beside Ash, wrapping my arm around her. "I'm so sorry."

Ash straightens one of Skadi's twisted braids. "She was too good for this evil world. I hope she finds peace among her friends."

I stiffen at the sound of gunfire somewhere in the outer sanctum.

Our heads swivel to the entrance where Sun Dreamer still stands. The dark Fae glances back at the fighting behind her, then turns to us. "I must leave now. If I don't see you again, take care. And Ash, in the future, do not be careless with your life. Even the undying can die."

Then Sun Dreamer blinks out into Som.

Her parting words still ring in my ears. And they make sense.

I grab Ash by the shoulders. "Let's get out of here. I don't care about killing Sindri. I just want you to be safe."

She stares at me, surprised. "You don't mean that. We have a duty—"

"I know, but listen to me. I met someone in Helheim who told me that love is also a duty. She's right. I didn't get that until now."

Ash's face shows a mix of excitement, worry, and confusion. "But where would we go?"

I turn to Tyler, who has been giving us space. "Can you take us into the past, back before Sindri rose to power in Norway?"

He reluctantly nods. "I can. But I'd still have to come back here to fight Sindri, even if it means doing it alone. I have to set this timeline straight. Think about it, Stefan, how many millions of couples like you and Ash never got to meet? What about their wasted love, killed in the cradle by Sindri's abuse of the timeline?"

Ash kisses me. "We can't let Tyler do it alone. And we can't let Skadi's sacrifice be in vain."

I shake my head. "No. Something will happen to you."

"I'll be careful, Stefan. I promise. But you have to be careful too."

The gunfire in the outer sanctum grows louder, and closer. Sounds like the resistance is losing the fight.

Ash grabs her pouch, pulls out the gate stones, and begins arranging them in an empty spot on the floor.

I still think this is a bad idea, but Ash wants to go, and I won't let her go without me.

Tyler puts a cautious hand on my shoulder. "Don't forget, we'll need the sword."

I nod a little sheepishly. "Hey, sorry about all that."

He smiles. "No worries. I get it. We're cool."

I turn to clockwork Gríma's pile of remains. Somehow, when I was attacking her, I managed not to cut Tyrfing's belt and scabbard. I retrieve them and cinch them around my waist.

I walk over to Tyrfing, lying dark and cold on the floor. I take a deep breath, steeling myself, and pick it up. The blade leaps to life, the brightness hurting my eyes.

Tyler studies me, speaking calmly, "You feel all right, Stefan?"

I nod. "I'm fine, but I'll keep it out of the scabbard until the job's done. Sun Dreamer said it takes a life when it's drawn. It did that when it killed Ash. I'm afraid if I sheathe it, then draw it again, it'll set the curse off, and I don't want it going after one of you."

Tyler nods. "Good thinking."

We join Ash as she finishes creating a circle of runes that spell out Svartalfheim.

She looks up at us. "It's ready."

Somewhere deep inside, my tactical mind crawls out of the cave where it's been hiding, and I find my command voice. "Tyler, swap out your revolver for one of the faecast rifles in your pouch."

He nods, fetching the weapon as I collect the faecast rifles and spare ammo from the fallen Svartr. I sling one of the rifles over my shoulder, and give the other to Ash.

I make strong eye contact with Ash and Tyler. "If either of you sees a mirror, shoot it without even thinking."

They both nod, looking determined.

I hear a bullet zing into the chamber, ricocheting off a wall. *We have to get out of here, now.*

I move into a balanced fighting stance, Tyrfing ready to strike. For all I know, something bad could be waiting on the other side.

"I'll go first. Then Ash, then Tyler."

I invoke and, without waiting for a response, step into the circle of gate stones.

# THE WORKSHOP

## TYLER BUCK

I WAIT MY TURN as Stefan steps into the circle of gate stones and disappears.

As Ash invokes and follows him, I catch movement in the corner of my eye. I turn to see a sentinel jamming his toady head through the entrance of the inner sanctum. His body won't fit through, despite his wiggling. His mirror eyes flash as they survey the chamber.

I fire my faecast rifle just as Ash steps into the circle.

One of the sentinel's eyes shatters with a bright crackle of energy and a hiss of steam.

My timesight isn't working on the creature, but I'm already stepping to the side, anticipating its tongue strike. The chained tongue whooshes past, just grazing my shoulder.

I fire again as I step into the gate stone circle. My bullet sparks inside the toad's open mouth as its tongue makes a second strike, and the chain wraps around me. Fortunately, I blink out of this world before the sentinel can reel me in.

Svartalfheim isn't what I expected. We're in a small room carved from stone and lit by glowing glass spheres in each corner. This chamber has four gold doors, one on each wall. Three of the doors have a red X smeared on them. It looks like it's written in blood.

Stefan stands guard with the shining sword while Ash kneels beside a slashed and battered body on the floor.

Ash looks up, grim-faced. "He's dead."

I glance at the body. He looks familiar. "Who is he?"

Ash swallows hard. "You."

Stunned, I take a step back.

Ash quickly collects the gate stones.

Stefan eyes me warily. "I thought you said you couldn't come back and risk running into yourself."

I feel my pulse racing. "I'd only risk it if the mission was a guaranteed failure without the jump. Also, I think that other Tyler must have known he was dying. There's a lot less risk if a living me encounters a dead me. Still, I need to be careful not to touch the body."

Stefan nods. "Looks like we owe you a thank-you. I think you were warning us not to try those three doors."

I nod, my mind going back to my Academy class on self-intervention. I'm in what they call a *loop*. It could be a closed loop, or an open loop. If it's a closed loop, I'm fucked. That means that as events progress, I will eventually have to come back to this room, paint the warnings in my blood, and die. Otherwise the mission will probably fail. If it's an open loop, and please let it be that, there's an exit point for me, and I might survive.

I study my alternate body lying on the floor. He's nude and doesn't appear to have his pouch, or his crystal claws. Man, things must have gone seriously sideways. I'm starting to feel sick inside.

Stefan looks at Ash and me as he points his blazing sword at the unmarked door. "Ready?"

We both nod, guns raised.

Stefan opens the door, revealing a corridor cut from solid rock, lit by an occasional glass sphere lying on the floor.

Stefan speaks quietly. "Change of formation. Tyler, you're back in the middle."

I nod as we enter the corridor. The air is thick and smells of brimstone. It stings my eyes a little but doesn't bother my lungs.

After only a minute of walking, the corridor opens into a vast, smoky cavern about a quarter mile across and hundreds of yards high. I've never seen such a massive underground space. Green and blue mosses glow on the walls, casting eerie light on the cavern floor a couple hundred feet below us.

In the center of the cavern floor sits a rectangular structure built of solid gold. The walls are decorated with thousands of big gems in every color of the rainbow. At one of the long ends of the rectangle, the one facing us, there's a wide double door that sparkles as if water is running over it. This has to be Sindri's palace.

We descend to the cavern floor on a long set of steps cut into the face of a steep stone slope.

The brimstone odor is no worse here than in the corridor, but something has changed. Sound isn't carrying as well, and our progress down the stairs is muffled.

Moving cautiously, we follow a path that leads to the gates of the golden palace. I'm shocked that we've seen no guards, or any other sign of life. Does that mean Sindri is confident no one can follow him here? But if that's true, why the four random doors of death where we first came in?

We stop at the palace's gold double doors. They have no handles. Their surfaces shimmer and move like a pond on a windy day, disrupting any reflections. There's something about those doors. They feel dangerous, like an electric fence.

Stefan turns to us. "Ideas?"

Ash cocks her head. "Maybe use the sword?"

I nod. "I agree with Ash, try Tyrfing. But be careful not to touch those doors. I got a bad feeling."

Stefan nods. "Agreed. Give me some space."

We step back. I hold my breath, ready for anything as Stefan presses the sword through one of the doors. The gold bubbles and melts in a stream that flows to the ground, and the shimmering effect disappears from both doors, leaving a flat, dull gold.

Tyrfing cuts through the door like a block of cheese, and soon Stefan has made a door within the door. The gold slab slams to the rock floor of the cavern, making less noise than it should.

I look at Ash and Stefan, both with their pointed wolf ears. "Is it just me, or is it quieter than it should be?"

Ash nods, puzzled. "It's not just you. It's like I'm wearing earplugs."

Stefan peers through the new opening in the door. "Yeah, that's weird, because it seems to work to our advantage. Let's go in and see if we can surprise him."

Stefan and Ash exchange a long look and something passes between them. She rests a gentle hand on his back as he steps through the hole, being careful not to touch the melted edges of his hand-carved door.

I follow Stefan and Ash inside the palace. I'm supposed to be in the middle of the column, but Ash seems to have changed the rules.

The sulphur smell is worse inside, and it's a lot warmer in here. I'm already hot-blooded, so I don't like the extra heat. I do much better in cold climates.

I don't know what I was expecting inside the palace, but this isn't it. The stone floor is filled with narrow shafts that belch smoke and hot air. The gold walls are engraved with mushrooms and insects. Silver, brass, and sindrion have been pounded into the grooves of the engravings to give them color and life. One large, glowing sphere hangs from the center of the entryway, but its light is weak and pale.

In a few random places, mushrooms and wildly twisting plants seem to grow in the stone floor. But they're all fake, made of metal pounded paper thin.

The entryway is empty. No people or guards. We pass through it, entering a narrow stone hallway.

A male dark elf, reading a piece of paper, rounds a corner and nearly crashes into us. Stefan takes his head off with

Tyrfing, never even breaking stride. It's the most casual killing I've ever seen.

Nearly losing Ash brought out something dark in Stefan. I can understand that. When all this is over, I hope he can let it go.

I stop to examine the head and body. The stocky dark elf wears only a loincloth and has a bit of gray in the dark hair above his pointed ears. The paper he was carrying now lies on the floor beside his body. Thanks to my gift of tongues, a graduation present from the Academy, I can read the Fae writing. There's a title at the top of the paper …

# ⊕(ᘜ ⊦ꓒ(ᘜ

It translates to *Slave Soup*. That's an ominous title. This paper contains a handwritten recipe. I don't have time to read all the ingredients. Was this dead Fae a cook? I guess that's possible. Are they eating slaves instead of animals?

The corridor takes us past a great feasting hall with a long gold table that seats dozens. Four human slaves are busy polishing the table and cleaning the floor. They don't notice us as we pass.

Steam drifts out into a hallway from a room ahead, and all I can think about is Sindri's clockwork monsters. There could be dozens of them in there.

Stefan approaches carefully, takes a peek inside, then gestures for us to follow him in.

Inside, we find a huge bath hall. Sindrion pipes emerge from the stone walls, pouring hot water into a twisting labyrinth of pools. Islands of plant life crowd the water, giving the place a tropical quality. I see a lot of squat trees with black bark and dark purple leaves.

A young female slave, holding a net on a pole, scoops purple leaves out of the steaming water. She looks up, eyes wide, ready to scream, but Stefan presses a finger to his lips and the girl falls silent.

Stefan whispers to Ash. "Find out if she knows where the workshop is, or if there's a part of the palace that's off-limits."

Ash uninvokes and approaches the trembling girl. They talk quietly for about a minute before Ash returns.

"She said there's a set of stairs farther down the hall and to the right. They lead down to a level where the slaves aren't allowed. She thinks the workshop is down there, but no one knows for sure. She's really scared. I don't think she'll tell them we're coming."

Stefan nods, giving the girl a warning look before leading us back out into the corridor. As Ash invokes, I glance back at the slave girl, her brown eyes wide with fear. I feel sorry for her, and part of me wants to save her. But I have a job to do.

As we continue down the hall, I realize we haven't seen one mirror or reflective surface in the palace. Even the bathhouse had moving water, covered with steam. No opportunities for Mirror Gríma to appear. That can't be an accident. It makes sense, I think. This is Sindri's turf; maybe he doesn't want Gríma nosing around. I feel more at ease already.

We find the set of stone steps and head down them. They open into a dark room with an orange glow. There's some sort of design on the floor, made of liquid lava.

On the other side of the lava we see a large faecast door, with two clockwork hounds standing guard. The beasts see us, and I hear faint growls, but they haven't attacked yet.

Stefan turns to us, whispering commands. "We do this quietly. Ash, hang back, firing only as a last resort. I'll use Tyrfing. Tyler, switch over to your crystal claws."

I nod, putting the rifle in my pouch and taking out my claws.

As Stefan and I approach the lava, I see the glowing design is not random. It's a map of North America. Is it purely decorative, or does it have a function?

The dogs charge, splitting up and approaching from both sides of the lava map. They aren't barking, which somehow makes them scarier. My timesight isn't working on them, and I'm convinced now that it's useless against clockwork creatures.

Fortunately, I've had some experience fighting animals. They tend to focus on offense, targeting the head, throat and gut.

My plan is to claw out those red clockwork eyes. Once the creature is blinded, I'll make short work of it.

About ten feet out, the hound leaps for my throat. Jumping from that far away is stupid, because it gives me plenty of time to react. On the ball of my right foot, I pivot back and to the side. As the dog flies past, I rake the right side of its head, gouging out its mechanical eye and tearing a panel off the side of its face.

The creature lands and skitters to a halt, metal paws seeking traction on the stone floor.

Before it can get its balance, I leap, grabbing it by the back legs. It must weigh a good two hundred pounds, but I'm pretty amped up right now, and I fling it into the lava map. With a final growl, it sinks to a molten death.

I look around for Stefan and find him beside me. He's already chopped his hound into several pieces and has come over to help me. Seeing my dog sink beneath the lava, he gives me a respectful tilt of his head. "Keep those claws on, for now."

I nod, enjoying the feel of them on my hands.

Ash moves to join us, and we approach the door on the far side of the room.

This door has a handle, and no shimmery magical effects. Stefan reaches up and opens it. The door is thick and heavy, made of what looks like brass.

We pass through the door, moving through a curved corridor. I smell meat cooking, like someone is having a barbecue.

The corridor opens into a wide, dimly lit room with a dozen small tables. Half-naked dark elf males sit at the tables, eating a meal.

Their heads turn toward us, ears twitching, the pupils in their amber eyes dilating.

Stefan calls to me over his shoulder. "Use your flashlight."

I scramble through my pouch as the dark Fae begin to rise from their tables. Fortunately, none of them appear to be armed.

I find my flashlight, switch it on, and sweep the room with it. The elves disappear with tiny shrieks, as if melted by the light. Interesting that they've chosen to run into Som rather than fight.

We've now lost our element of surprise, but we may still have some time. Things move slowly in Som. A minute here is only a couple of seconds there.

As we search the mess hall, Ash points out that the tables are all supported by square structures. None of us think Sindri would hide his heart box here, but we have to be sure.

Stefan uses Tyrfing to cut through the tables on a diagonal, so the top halves fall away under their own weight.

The squares under the tables turn out to be solid blocks of stone. None of them have a poisonous little elf heart inside.

We find a kitchen adjacent to the mess hall, and give it a quick search. At the back of the kitchen I find the source of the barbecue smell. Ash sees it too, and we both end up vomiting.

A dead slave, probably a middle-aged man, turns slowly on an automated roasting spit. His stomach has been cut open, emptied out, stuffed to bulging with spices and God knows what, and then sewn shut.

Stefan finds us spitting and wiping our faces. His eyes pass over the roasted human, but he doesn't react. Man, if this doesn't bother him, he must have seen some bad shit.

There's nothing box-shaped in the kitchen, so we move on to another corridor on the far side of the cafeteria.

The hallway leads us into an empty workshop, filled with workstations and tools, and hundreds of gears, cog wheels, and other mechanical parts.

There's no one here. Is this Sindri's workshop? If so, there's no sign of him. Is he in Som?

We search the workshop, expecting trouble, but nothing attacks us. Stefan finds a locked box. He cuts it open, but there are only clockwork parts inside, a batch of red mechanical eyes.

After giving up on the workshop, we exit via a set of descending stairs. The farther down we go, the wider the stairs become, and then they split, curling around a dark hole in the middle, about twenty feet across.

We cut to the right as we pass the hole. It's like the small shafts upstairs in the entryway, but on a grander scale. A hot wind blows up from the shaft, and none of us wants to lean over and look down inside.

The stairs seem to go on forever, then suddenly, they open into a huge hallway about fifty feet across and maybe forty feet high.

I realize this space is big enough to accommodate my dragon form. For a moment, that gives me comfort. Then I realize it's also big enough to accommodate a clockwork dragon. Last I heard, Sindri wanted to study me because he was having trouble with his prototype. I hope it isn't functional yet.

At the end of the massive hallway stands an immense double door made of sindrion. Fae metal is light, but those doors are so huge I'll bet they weigh several tons.

Looking at those towering doors, I'm convinced that Sindri is on the other side. The city under the mountain is called Dragonworks, but I'm guessing this is the *real* Dragonworks, where Sindri is building his clockwork dragon.

Seeing the faces of Stefan and Ash, I can tell they're thinking the same thing.

As we approach the colossal doors, we see an open arch, about ten feet high, on the left side of the wide hallway.

Stefan peeks through the arch, then signals us to follow him in.

This room has the look of a private chamber. It has a toilet, several tables heaped with mechanical parts, and a desk scattered with books.

The walls here are veined. Thin streams of lava flow through them, creating intricate geometric patterns that form and then disperse. I have no idea why the lava doesn't spill out onto the floor.

We search the room. I examine the books on the desk. They're printed books! I was expecting something handwritten. All are written in a Fae language and cover technical subjects such as mathematics and engineering.

Ash joins me and checks out the books. "There's no bed here. I think this room is his study."

Stefan stands at the toilet, frowning. "No bed makes sense. A clockwork creature doesn't need sleep. But it needs a toilet?"

Ash nods, in sync with his thinking. "You're wondering if that's where he hides his heart."

Stefan nods, then reaches over and pulls a chain on the wall near the toilet. "It didn't flush."

Suddenly, the floor shakes and a deep rumble fills the thick air.

I race over to the archway and look down the hall. The giant doors are slowly moving outward. Through the growing crack between the doors, I see the green metallic face of a clockwork dragon.

Shit, the party's on!

I duck back into the study to warn the others. "It's a clockwork dragon. If you fight it, you'll die, so let me deal with it. You two stay here and find that heart."

I drop my crystal claws into my pouch and toss the pouch to Ash.

Outside, the clockwork dragon roars, and the sound rattles my teeth.

Stefan looks concerned. "We can give you fire support."

I shake my head. "If that dragon has flames, he'll burn you to your bones. One blast, and you're both gone. Please, just find that heart and finish off Sindri. Then we can all get out of here."

Stefan reluctantly nods. "Okay. Good luck, Tyler."

Ash hugs me, whispering in my ear, "Be careful. The world needs you."

I nod, avoiding her eyes, trying to stay cool and collected.

In three long strides I'm through the archway and shifting into my dragon form. I didn't take the time to undress first, so my clothes are getting torn up.

My skin burns, and I feel the familiar anger of my dragon.

The green dragon's first blast hits me before I finish my transformation. That's actually good, because the damage heals as I finish shifting. It was a hot, dry flame, unlike my liquid fire, and not as effective.

The doors are nearly open when I face off against the beast, standing fifteen feet beyond the entryway. It has amber eyes that burn like lighthouses, rows of sharp teeth jammed together like shiny missiles, and clenching claws gouging grooves in the stone floor.

It launches its second fire blast simultaneous to mine. This time, I feel very little heat. My blast pushes through to its neck, and liquid fire drips from its green sindrion scales. I don't see any damage at all. Fire attacks aren't going to help either of us.

I think back to my early training, when I first became a dracoform. My emerald mentor, Lagashan, taught me how to fight in dragon form. I have numerous weapons besides fire, such as fore and rear claws, fangs, and a whipping tail. I also have small horns I can use to butt or gore enemies. The last weapon is my size. I can crush things with my bulk. But I doubt that will be much help here.

Lagashan also taught me defense, how to protect my vulnerable areas: eyes, open mouth, wings, and belly. I have a feeling her training is about to come in handy, especially since timesight isn't working against this creature.

Let's see what this clockwork bastard is made of. I lower my head, charging the creature with my horns.

I pass through the gates, and in my peripheral vision, I see a vast work area with a scaffolding. This is definitely Sindri's workshop, the place where he built this clockwork dragon.

A split second before impact, the metal dragon lowers its head, and our skulls collide with a thunderclap. It doesn't have horns, but the creature is damned heavy and it feels like running into a wall. One of my horns breaks off and tumbles to the floor, but the injury doesn't hurt.

Wow, I wasn't expecting that.

For some reason, the creature suddenly turns, exposing its flank to me. That doesn't seem like a smart move. I see now that the dragon's wings are little more than stubs. The wings are probably the trickiest part, and Sindri never finished them.

I now realize why the dragon turned aside. A green clockwork elf, complete with pointed ears, sits in a harness on the dragon's back. This *has* to be Sindri. His red eyes glow as he raises two faecast pistols and fires.

I barely move my head away in time. One shot misses, but the other catches me square in the throat, punching through my scales and drawing blood.

I don't think I'm dying, but I'm hurt, and I'm already having trouble breathing.

I turn to the side, whipping my tail as Sindri fires twice more, hitting me in the left flank and wing.

My tail strikes Sindri hard, flinging him from the saddle. He flies across the room. One of his pistols clatters to the floor, but he manages to hold on to the other one as he bounces off a wall and plunges into a channel of lava flowing around the perimeter of the workshop.

So much for Sindri. Now I have to kill his beast.

The creature has slowed, as if confused by the loss of its rider.

As I bite down on its metallic neck, I feel a stabbing pain from the bullet wound in my side. I'm also feeling dizzy from blood loss and breathing problems.

I feel my teeth break as my jaws tighten around the neck of the clockwork creature. Unlike my horn, my broken teeth hurt like hell, and the pain blurs my vision.

The creature snaps its head back to bite the side of my face, but it's not flexible enough to pull off the move.

I flap, my left wing in agony, and get enough air to straddle the dragon's back, then I reach around with my foreclaws and tear out its lighthouse eyes.

The metallic beast, feeling no pain, fails to react as I hoped. It simply spins around, now belly to belly, and begins fighting with tooth and claw.

I see now that several of my foreclaws are broken. Before I realize it, my neck is in the creature's jaws, and the claws of its rear leg have torn off half my right wing.

Pain washes through me like a powerful drug. My vision goes dark and I can't breathe.

With what's left of my wings, I manage to get enough lift to bring both rear claws up on the dragon's gut. My rear claws are *strong*, and I feel the dragon's metal scales tearing away as I dig into its belly.

It must have let go of my neck, because I can wheeze in a thin stream of air. My vision returns, though dimmer than before.

Steam pours from the creature's mouth, and its jaws clench in random spasms.

With its eyes gone, it can't see me as I grab its head in my foreclaws and twist.

Its metal neck groans, crackles, and then breaks.

The creature collapses beneath me, jaws still snapping as it twitches in its death throes.

I stumble away from the dying beast, lucky to be alive. If that thing had been built right and taught to fight properly, I wouldn't have stood a chance.

Now free of my adversary, I get a better look at the workshop. There are actually two scaffoldings here, one empty, and another with a smaller, half-built dragon. I wonder if that was his first attempt, and he abandoned it.

A bubbling sound catches my ear and I turn slowly, feeling terrible pain from my wounds.

I thought the fight was over, but it isn't.

Clockwork Sindri rises from the lava, raises a pistol, and fires.

How he and the pistol survived the lava, I'll never understand.

I lower my head and empty the last of my flame reserve, for all the good it will do. The bullet catches my good horn, shattering it as well.

Sindri shuffles forward, out of the lava, with my liquid flames dripping off him.

He fires twice more, hitting me in the mouth and front leg. Without timesight, I don't even see it coming.

I go down hard, gurgling blood. I try to use my back legs to propel myself toward him, but I can't feel them anymore.

I decide to play dead. If he turns his attention away from me, I can shift back to human form, healing my wounds. I don't have my crystal claws, but I do remember where he dropped that faecast pistol when I knocked him off his dragon.

Sindri approaches, haltingly, gears grinding in his legs.

I watch him through slitted eyes. Is he buying my act?

He suddenly aims the pistol at my head and pulls the trigger.

Nothing happens.

Hah, the fucker is out of bullets! I would laugh, but I'm supposed to be playing dead.

He tosses the empty weapon, then starts looking around for the pistol he dropped earlier.

Suddenly, down the corridor, back in the study, I hear Ash scream in horror. Something's gone wrong in there!

Sindri's head snaps around and he moves toward the scream. He pauses at his dead dragon, then bends down and detaches two of its razor claws. Sindri somehow connects the claws to his mechanical hands, then shambles through the open gates and down the hall toward the study.

Goddammit. Ash and Stefan are in trouble, and resurrected Sindri with his claw hands is the last thing they need.

I shift back to human form. The devastating pain leaves my body as the wounds heal.

Now nude, I scramble to where I thought Sindri dropped the loaded pistol, but it isn't there.

Shit, what happened to it?

Realizing that my perspective was different in dragon form, I mentally correct for my human height and continue the search.

I spot a shimmer as the glowing lava reflects on the pistol handle. I grab the gun, turning toward the open doors just as Sindri approaches the study, his claws spinning like a blender.

# Everyone I Love

## ASH KINLEY

I watch Stefan use Tyrfing to cut through the toilet. Sure enough, inside the base of the toilet rests a silver box, shimmering the same way as the doors to the palace entrance.

I feel a surge of hope. "That's it! That's gotta be it!"

Stefan nods, keeping his emotions in check.

Somewhere down the hallway a terrible battle rages. The floor beneath us trembles as painful metallic noises jangle my ears and jolt my bones.

I know in my heart that Tyler's in trouble. We have to take out Sindri, and we have to do it *now*.

Stefan, realizing this is no time for finesse, lifts Tyrfing high and brings it down hard on the box. The air whistles with the passing blade and the box screeches as the sword passes through it. Blood spurts from the box and the severed heart inside it makes a loud sighing noise.

Adrenaline surges through me as Stefan slips Tyrfing into the silver scabbard at his waist. He turns to me and reaches for Tyler's pouch. "I'll get the Devourer."

The thought of Stefan touching that scary skull fills me with terror. I just *know* something will go wrong.

I pull the pouch away from him. "No, I'll do this part."

Stefan's eyes are hard. "Dammit, Ash, you already got killed. You've taken enough risks. I'm doing this."

I want to reach into the pouch and grab the Devourer before Stefan can take it. But my will weakens under Stefan's powerful stare. I've never seen him more commanding.

I hand the pouch over with a trembling hand. "Please, please, please be careful."

He nods, all business, as he opens the pouch and removes the Devourer, wrapped in the space blanket.

He pulls away the blanket, revealing the horrible jeweled skull. Some of the jewels wink, and suddenly, a spectral tongue emerges from its bony jaws and licks the blood from a cut on Stefan's hand.

A scream bursts from my lungs as the skull takes to the air, circling Stefan, its teeth chomping like a wood chipper.

I raise my gun to fire at it, but Stefan knocks my barrel aside.

*What's wrong with him?*

The skull moves away from Stefan, searching the room like a dog following a scent trail. In a few moments, it finds the silver box and licks the severed heart with its ghostly tongue.

I step over to Stefan, who wipes the blood from his hand. "What happened? Are you all right?"

He nods. "It wasn't my blood. Splashback from the heart."

*I thought he was cut, but I see now his hand is unblemished.* "Oh, thank God!"

I embrace him, and we watch as the Devourer makes keening noises as it gulps down bits of heart like a dog swallowing treats.

Behind us, something whirs. Stefan and I turn to see a clockwork dark elf with glowing red eyes. Huge curved blades spin on his hands. This must be Sindri!

But before we can shoot, Sindri's head snaps to the side, hit by multiple blasts of gunfire. Pieces of his head fly away, revealing an array of steaming gizmos.

Sindri loses control of his body. He jerks and spins, his whirling blades breaking off onto the stone wall. Then he falls with a clatter, sending a gear wheeling across the floor.

Tyler appears in the doorway, nude, with a faecast pistol in his hand. "Hey, sorry, he kind of got away from me. Everyone okay in here?"

I look back at the Devourer. It hisses in satisfaction as it finishes its bloody meal, then disappears with a loud pop. The gems that were embedded in the skull scatter across the floor.

Then suddenly, everything changes, and I gasp in surprise.

I'm standing under a night sky in medieval Norway, holding hands with Stefan and Tyler.

I remember this moment. We had just killed Gríma at the Jotunborg. I had met Seeker, and we were making a time jump back to Corby.

Tyler was naked a second ago, but he's dressed now. We're wearing the same clothes we had back in Norway. Stefan no longer has Tyrfing at his side, and I don't feel the weight of the gate stones in my pouch.

Tyler sees the surprise on my face and speaks in a calm, professional tone. "Okay, my friends, looks like we're experiencing a temporal correction. That's a good thing. How much do you each remember?"

I find my voice. "All of it, I think."

Stefan nods. "Me too."

Tyler mulls it over. "That's unusual, but it makes sense. Each of you played an integral role in repairing the line. We're supposed to jump to the present now, to Corby. I'm hoping everything will be normal there."

*Something's been bothering me and I have to ask.* "What about Gríma? Is she really dead, or will she be in the present when we get there?"

"She's dead. I remember killing her with my fire at the Jotunborg. This correction is taking place *after* her death, not before, so her fate can't be rewritten. I suspect it was Sindri who resurrected her, and he's gone now, so I don't expect to see Mirror Gríma when we get home."

I nod sadly, realizing what that means. "So anyone who died before this correction is still dead, including Magnus?"

"I'm afraid so."

*Poor Magnus. I wish we could have helped him.*

Stefan lets go of our hands and checks his arm. "That made me think of Mahna. I used to have scars where she carved her name in me. They're gone now, so hopefully she won't screw up the jump."

Tyler nods, looking a little worried. "That *is* good news about Mahna, but we're still not out of danger. I took some damage in that first jump, and when they repaired it, they messed me up a little. My accuracy's off."

*I'm confused.* "If the timeline is fixed, doesn't that mean the jump that Mahna interrupted never actually happened?"

Tyler nods. "You're right, but it was a metaphysical injury. Part of my soul was damaged and they cut it away. I only have one soul, and it exists simultaneously on all alternate timelines. That's how we were able to take out Sindri, because the Devourer destroyed his soul. In fact, the three of us are the only ones who will remember Sindri. To everyone else, he never existed."

Stefan takes our hands. "I'm getting a headache. Let's jump. I want to see Corby again."

Tyler turns to me and I give him a nod.

He takes a deep breath, and suddenly it feels like we're falling.

A few moments later, I see the vague outline of a city forming around us. This is wrong. There shouldn't be a city outside of Corby. This jump is taking forever. I think Tyler is having trouble getting us back to the right time period.

My stomach lurches. What if we can't get home? I squeeze Stefan's hand. I'll be okay living anywhere, as long as we're together.

The shadowy city disappears, eventually replaced by a shrouded forest that becomes more distinct as we emerge from the jump.

This time, when the jump is over, Tyler is still conscious. He looks tired, but he's smiling as he releases our hands. "I think we made it."

The air smells like fall leaves and pine needles. There's no trace of smoke.

Stefan turns to me. "Check the time compass. See if the rift is gone."

I take the compass from my pouch. The silver needle isn't moving. "Looks good."

Tyler pulls his phone from his pouch. "I've got a signal. Give me a minute to report in with my bureau chief."

As Tyler talks on the phone, Stefan and I use the time to hug and kiss. It feels so good to hold him in my arms. I'm going to have nightmares about the Devourer licking that blood from his hand. I thought I had lost him. It was a horrible feeling, one that I never want to have again.

Stefan responds to the pain in my face, trying to lighten the mood. "Hey, someone still owes you a steak dinner."

*Wow, that seems like a lifetime ago.*

I smile. "I'm in, as long as Celia won't be joining us. I still can't believe she showed up at your house and just took off her clothes."

He smiles apologetically, "From now on, you're the only one who's allowed to do that."

"That's right, mister. Don't you forget it."

Tyler, now off the phone, approaches us with a sad face. "I've confirmed it with my chief. The timeline's been completely repaired."

*Then why does he look upset?* "That's good news, isn't it?"

"Yeah, but this is a big deal at Specta Aeternal. They want to debrief me, *right now*. And besides the debriefing, they're having an internal problem that I need to look into. They're picking me up in a few minutes. And after that, I'm scheduled for metaphysical therapy. I was really hoping to hang with you guys for a while, but that just isn't in the cards."

I feel a tug at my heart. "Promise you'll come back when you can. You're always welcome here."

"Thanks, I'll try. When I tell SA about all your help, they'll be thankful. If either of you ever needs a favor from us, you'll get it."

Stefan extends his hand to Tyler. "You've got a damned impressive skill set. Glad you're on our side."

Tyler smiles and they exchange a handshake hug.

I embrace Tyler, feeling the dragon heat in his body, and whisper in his ear. "This Rosemarie, I hope you can get back together with her."

He nods. "Me too."

I sit at a table in the butterfly-themed kitchen belonging to Stefan's mother. His parents will be back from the hospital tomorrow, so it's the last night we'll have use of the house.

It's hard to believe that no time has passed here while we were gone. The battle against KoR at Fort Adams was only two days ago. The people here in Corby are still reeling from their losses.

And it was only last night that I came here for my first date with Stefan, found Celia in her underwear, and then ran when the cops showed up.

Stefan puts two hot steaks on a pair of plates. He used his mother's technique of searing them in a skillet before finishing them in the oven.

I rub my hands together. "God, those smell good."

He puts the plates on the table and I pat his leg with my hand. It's nice to be alone together, where I can just touch him whenever, for no reason.

He leans over and kisses me. "There's baked potatoes too. Just give me a minute."

*Something tells me this is going to be the best meal of my life.*

Then the doorbell rings.

I huff. "If that's Celia, I'll …"

Stefan calls out, "Who is it?"

A strong voice responds, "Vermont State Police."

I stiffen. *They're back!*

Last time they came, I ran. I knew they wanted me for my father's death. But now I'm not so sure. When I met Mom in Helheim, she said she took the rap for me. Is that true? Was my encounter with her even real?

Stefan squeezes my shoulder. "How do you want to handle it?"

I'm tired of running, and angry that someone's ruining my first real dinner with Stefan. "I'll deal with it."

I give him one last kiss, then march to the door and throw it open.

"I'm Ash Kinley. You looking for me?"

The burly trooper is surprised. "Actually, yeah. Hey, aren't you the one who ran off last night?"

Shaking off my nerves, I look him in the eye. "Well, you got me now. What's up?"

"About a week back, a kid in Elmore found a couple of freaked-out dogs, said they smelled like smoke. He was keeping them in a shed until his mother found out. One of them had a chip with your name, and an address for a house up on the ridge here, but nobody answered the door."

My heart pounds as goose bumps rise on my arms. He's talking about Sigrid's house. She must have chipped Lucky before she gave him to me!

I speak through a lump in my throat. "My dogs are still alive?"

He nods. "Yeah, they're sleeping in my rig's cargo bay."

He pushes a button on his key fob, and the hatch lifts on the back of his dark green State Police SUV.

I hold my breath, both hands over my heart.

Two dogs jump out of the SUV: Shasta, my shy husky, and Lucky, my floppy-eared Anatolian pup.

I can't believe it! I was looking for them in medieval Norway, and they were here all along.

I burst into tears as I sit on the porch and the happy dogs leap into my arms. "I missed you both so much!"

Stefan shakes hands with the cop and thanks him, and I nod my thanks through a frenzy of dog licks.

The trooper leaves, giving me and the dogs a final smile before pulling away in his SUV.

I blubber like a fool as the dogs snuggle against me.

Stefan sits on the porch beside me. "You okay?"

I pull him into my happy reunion with the dogs. "I'm more than okay. I'm the happiest I've ever been. Everyone I love is here in one place."

Stefan smiles and puts his arm around me. We sit together on the porch, petting the dogs and watching the moon rise over the trees. The food in the kitchen can wait. I just want to enjoy this feeling.

The Orion constellation is overhead. Of course, the wolf's eye is missing, but if I squint just right, I can see it there.

All my anger and fears are gone. I won't let myself be a product of what my father and Gríma did to me. I am a product of this perfect moment, with these sweet animals, and the loving man I'll share the rest of my life with.

# BONUSES

Respected Reader,

This is your author, Shay Roberts. You have reached the end of the book. I hope you enjoyed it.

To read more about Stefan, check out Emma's Saga: http://shayroberts.com/books/vampire-soul/

To read more about Tyler, check out Tyler's Saga: http://shayroberts.com/books/dragon-blood/

As a thank-you for reading *Werewolf Undying*, please go to http://shayroberts.com/undyingbonus to get the following free gifts ...

- ♥ *Werewolf Undying* jigsaw and slider puzzles.
- ♥ An option to vote if you want more books in this series.
- ♥ Updates, and a newsletter with occasional reader discounts and giveaways.

Please accept these gifts with no obligation by visiting: http://shayroberts.com/undyingbonus

Happiness is a good book!

Your personal scribe,

~ Shay ~

# Acknowledgments

It takes a lot of great people to make a great book. Thank you, one and all.

*Afiya, Cathy Pontious, Damian Southam, Eliza Dee, Elizabeth M. Meadows, Isabella Le Roux, Joyce E.S. Kelly, Katherine Tomlinson, Kathie Middlemiss, Kathy Knuckles, Kim Pettit, Leila Roberts, Loralei, Lyla Roberts, Margaret Cambridge, Marina Elez, Merrie Weiler, Monique Godin, Pamela Davis, Rebecca Brown, Renata Gill, Ryan W. Schukei, Silvia Pascale, Susan Reeve, Teresa S., Veronica McIntyre, and Wendy Wright.*

Made in the USA
Columbia, SC
22 April 2019